AWAKE AGAIN

SUSAN HATTON

SUSAN HATTON

Copyright © Susan Hatton 2014

The author or authors assert their moral right under the Copyright, Designs and Patents Act, 1988, to be identified as the author or authors of this work.

All Rights reserved. No part of this publication may be reproduced, copied, stored in a retrieval system, or transmitted, in any form or by any means, without the prior written consent of the author or publisher, nor be otherwise circulated in any form of binding or cover other than that in which it is published and without a similar condition being imposed on the subsequent purchaser.

AWAKE AGAIN

Thank you to my friends for believing in me and helping when it was needed, and to those who didn't believe in me for pushing harder.

SUSAN HATTON

<u>Chapter 1</u>

The concrete beneath my head is hard and cold and I think there is a bruise on the cheek I'm resting on. Slowly, I attempt to turn my head to ease the stinging sensation, and a shooting pain roars through my skull like white hot lightening lasting only a few seconds, telling me instantly how this woman died. The agony of this body is indescribable but I force myself not to scream. I merely gasp in surprise as my body heals itself, eyes jolting open to assess my surroundings. My lungs automatically pulling in a large breath of air even though I don't need it, it's just what this mortal body is used to. I lift my hand to rub my head hoping for some kind of release from the dull ache left behind, and I'm covered in blood.

I sense no danger lurking in the alley way I'm lying in and turn onto my back looking at the neglected and abandoned buildings surrounding me, attempting to ignore this new body's pain as I try to make sense of the world I find myself in now.

As my body heals it begins to change and transform. I stare into the cloudless night's sky, welcoming the familiarity of the darkness. Taking comfort in the fact that I will soon enough be back within natures solid embrace waiting in comfort and safety for the new life I deserve, the life I have been promised as a reward for my torturous time defending this wretched world. My thoughts are leading me to a dark place, a place which I don't wish to go right now, and I force myself to focus on the now instead of the past or future.

I delve into the memories left within the mind of this body. Learning about the world and accustoming myself to my new surroundings within a few moments. I learn about mobile telephones, the internet, cars and even suitable social skills all without leaving the alleyway.

My skin tingles as it becomes stronger, the pain subsiding as the wounds that led to this woman's death heal completely. I send a thank you prayer and hope she reaches a peaceful after life. It's the least I can do for her, my purpose here has meant me taking over her body after her soul departed.

The woman's name who inhabited this body before me was Veronica. I relax into the change, hidden within the darkness of night, her story unravelling before my very eyes.

I sift through her memories one image and emotion at a time. Pictures of her growing up and starting her own family mingled with pictures of her being tormented at school as other kids throw food at her. She had lost her mother at a young age and after a few years her father found solace with a male partner. Veronica was brought up in a very loving and nurturing environment. The other children at school however bullied her more for having two fathers, I see the pictures in my head of them abusing Veronica as though it is happening to me and I begin to feel anger.

I don't understand why having two fathers made her a target for bullying, or why anyone would be a target for that matter. Just because somebody has different colour hair or eyes, or spaces in their teeth, or even if they prefer someone of the same sex to the opposite, it doesn't give anyone the right to put them down. Nobody has the right to manipulate another person's emotions into not feeling adequate.

Her memories swiftly change into an image of Veronica in a beautiful ball gown with a few girls the same age at her sides, the word prom flashes in my mind and although I have no inclination as to what it means a small smile spreads on my lips, it must be an emotion planted from Veronica's subconscious. The image again switches to the same group of girls sitting around a table in multi-coloured cocktail dresses, glasses of wine raised towards a stunning Veronica wearing an elegant white dress, as I watch her husband leans over and kisses her cheek with a look of absolute adoration twinkling in his eyes.

The memories move again and I am watching a short clip from a funeral, I believe it to be one of her fathers from how hard she is crying, her husband from the previous memory stroking her back. The next memory is of Veronica and her husband viewing a home together and Veronica stroking her swollen tummy, caressing her unborn child, who swims into view as yet again the memory changes. Only the child is watching her walk out with her bags packed, tears streaming down all of their faces. She is leaving? Her emotions are still very clear and I feel myself actually get caught in the moment, wanting to shout her back but before I open my mouth everything changes again.

I see Veronica in a flat with empty bottles surrounding her. Other girls are trying to wake her up by kicking her, and when she moves they merely shrug and walk away to get ready for their shift on the streets. They were only checking she wasn't dead! I wonder how she could have switched lives so drastically.

A respectable high class woman like Veronica, suddenly living off the streets. The alcohol addiction seems to have started when she lost her father, and all I can gather is that she left because it was tearing the family apart.

It is all so confusing being shown images and clips from her life and trying to piece together the information, thankfully Veronica's emotions were so strong and powerful that they are still evident.

A clip in my head plays of her; leaning her hip against a large building while smoking a cigarette and rubbing her blistered foot inside a red high heel shoe. I feel those heels on my feet right now and I focus more on this memory, knowing it will show me how she died.

Standing, she began the walk yet again feeling weak and tired, limping slightly on her worse foot but trying her best not to show it. Her feet are hardening against the blisters and sores from wearing heels all night every night, but they still hurt a lot. People would walk the street and yell abuse at her, boys on their way home from the clubs would whistle at her cheaply. She keeps her false smile and waves it off, though it wounds her deep inside.

I see a clip of her learning about working the streets from the girls already out there, the ones who used to laugh and sneer at her well groomed appearance.

"You got to make them want to stop for you, show some skin and shimmy when you walk. Moving your hips when you're walking makes them think how you would move them in sex."

"Chew gum, keeps your breath fresh and makes them look at your mouth, every bloke loves fucking a girl's mouth!"

"If they hit you to the ground you just curl up in a ball and wait for them to get it out there system, if they try to not pay you scream rape."

"Always have plenty of condoms in your bag, as well as chewing gum."

"Tissues too if you can or wet wipes even. You gotta be clean for the next customer!" The girls bombarded her with tips and she tried to take note of everything.

She packed her small clutch bag for work with condoms, chewing gum, hand sanitizer, tooth brush and paste, spare panties, make up and a comb. Ready for a nights work.

After what felt like a lifetime to Veronica a dark red car sounding like it's about to give out pulled up a little way in front of her. The license plate read 3IG D1K.

She shimmied her hips over to the passenger window and cringed as the glass rolled down, revealing the stench of old fast food and stale tobacco smoke, confirming a customer. At last!

"What can I do you for handsome?" she asked in her husky work voice with a promising and seductive smile on her face, she had just put a fresh piece of chewing gum in her mouth so he would pick up on the scent of mint and start thinking about her mouth, just as the girls had told her to a few months ago only now she did it out of habit.

After a while talking to the driver, a man with blonde unkempt hair, spotty face and looking extremely unclean, he had talked her price down by almost half! Begrudgingly, Veronica accepted as it seemed he was the only customer she was going to get tonight.

When he climbed out of the car she noticed him

stumbling and babbling about a 'crazy bitch' and how he 'taught her a lesson' and she took this as a warning to be extra polite considering he is already very drunk and slightly angry.

"This way handsome, I'll take care of you." she led him down the alley way where she always did her business, and behind the bins so nobody from the street could see them. The smell of whiskey making her cringe but at least it covered the smell of the overflowing bins next to them.

She positioned him against the wall and began with the usual protocol. Unbuttoning his trousers with one hand and rubbing her other over the bulge at the front. He was already aroused before she had even touched him and at least she knew he wouldn't take long. His smile was creepy and lopsided, she tried to focus on anything else around her as he kept trying to kiss her on the lips and push his hips forward so she was rubbing him harder. He was most definitely not a patient customer.

"Yeah baby, come on hurry up babe." His breath wreaked of tobacco and weed, it was almost enough to make her sick. He moves his arms out to grab her and hold her against him but he almost falls on top of her laughing, she had to push him back against the wall where he slumped over chuckling, hands on his knees and looking about ready to collapse.

"Money first, *baby!*" she said to him, sneering at the last word. She hated her customers calling her baby.

"Oh come on babe don't be like that, I got your money right here." he opened his trousers and pulled out his penis, laughing as though it was some kind of private joke, he seems to think the act makes him irresistible. Veronica was about to tell him to pay up or he wouldn't get the services he wanted when she noticed his penis looking a rather worrying colour, welts and blisters covering the disgustingly warped appendage.

"Deals off, you need to see a doctor." she turned to walk away towards a club at the end of the alley way to freshen up, pulling out the hand sanitizer in the small bag hanging off her shoulder. Just the sight of him enough to make her feel more unclean than if she had actually had sex with a regular customer.

"You fucking bitch get back here." His hand on her shoulder yanked her back aggressively. "You don't fucking walk away from me!" he yelled after her, grabbing her again from behind and pushing her down onto the floor. He began kicking her while she curled up just like the girls had told her to, bringing her knees up to protect her ribs after the first blow took her breath away. She felt the bruises forming over her breasts already. Her bottle of hand sanitizer emptied onto the concrete floor of the alley way while she yelped in pain. The rest of the contents of her bag had spilled out as it crashed to the floor.

When the blows stopped she heard his footsteps walking slowly around her, then she felt his hand in her hair as he pulled her head up harshly to look at him. She screamed in agony as a sharp pain shot through her neck leaving the trail feeling hot and burnt. Her scream however was unheard as they were alone in the alleyway, the music from the club covering any noise on the street a few feet away.

"Now we have a little problem here, I'm one very angry customer." he says through gritted teeth, spit flying at her face. His voice was menacingly low and it caused her heart to race in fear as she tried desperately not give in to the floods of tears about to break through. "And I think there is something you can do to satisfy my needs. You see I was promised satisfaction and I ain't... Fucking... Had it!" a shiver ran down her spine as she knew what to expect next.

The girls had warned her that now and then you would get the odd customer trying to act hard and scare her into a free service. She was mentally prepared, though it still came as a major shock to the system, and she shook with fear. Trying to hide it she looked into his face with as much courage as she could find, trying to reassure herself that she was going to be OK.

"Now, when I put my dick in your mouth you're going to suck it. That's right baby I want you to suck it and then I want you to fuck it. And if you dare bite down on it I promise you now you *will* be sorry. Do you understand me baby?" As she was about to spit in his face and make a run for it something touched her neck. It was cold, solid and extremely sharp. A knife! A whole new fear grabbed her heart, and I feel the cold twinge of panic as though it is happening to me.

"Yes." she whispered to him quietly. She couldn't move her head, her voice was shaking and tears were flooding down her face as she tried to nod without piercing her skin on the knife still pressed firmly against her flesh.

He smiled at her cruelly and she noticed some of his teeth were missing; she tried to get a good look so she could report him later to the police, knowing to check for tattoos, scars and hair and eye colour etc. But for some reason her mind went blank!

She couldn't tell the colour of his eyes. Are they green or blue? He has blonde messy hair. His trousers are blue denim and his shirt is black, no distinguishing design or logos, he is wearing white trainers with simple white laces that in all honesty look as though they are older than he is!

While Veronica was too much in shock to notice anything, I make sure to notice the scar on his cheek and the words *FUCK* and *LOVE* tattooed on his knuckles.

He stood back up without letting go of her hair and took his penis out of his trousers again, placing the tip at her mouth. The vile smell of infection reached her nose, and she gagged at the thought. But when she opened her mouth to be sick he thrust his hips forward and forced himself into her mouth. He was groaning with pleasure as she was fighting to get away.

He forced himself inside her mouth so far she gagged and struggled to breathe, harder and harder he thrust his hips as she continued to try fighting against him. His hand still in her hair, pulling clumps of it out at the roots as she fought so violently. Still aware of the knife at her throat she avoided biting down as much as she could, but she could feel the bumps on her gums from his warts and she wretched horrifically.

All she could think about was getting away from him, the tears burned her eyes much like mine are now watching the horrific scene and I can't bring myself to stop. The pain in her mouth was becoming unbearable. There was nothing else she could focus on. As I watch this monstrous scene being played out in front of me right now I cry to myself, feeling what she felt and the emotions she experienced. The agony not only physical, but knowing she had put herself in a position to be abused so easily feeling like vinegar in her wounds.

"Oh yeah baby I like it when they fight." Her hands searched for the knife he had moments before held to her throat but she couldn't feel a thing. He thrust into her mouth brutally with his head back in pleasure. She was choking, gagging, tasting her own vomit as the violent action aggravated her gag reflex and caused her to wretch over and over. Her knees blooded and bruised from the concrete beneath them but she was unable to move or stand up by the hand in her hair holding her down. Franticly she tried to pull away and harder and harder he pulled her back. She was in so much excruciating pain at that point from the viscous attack in her mouth and the bruises across her ribs from the kicking moments before, that she found herself wishing he *would* kill her, just to make it all stop.

His words were becoming more violent, calling her names as he grabbed the sides of her head with both hands forcing her onto him harder and groaning out loud as she began screaming. "Yeah that's it you fucking dirty bitch, ain't gonna turn your back on me again are ya." I cringe at the language this monster uses.

He carried on like that for nearly twenty minutes, Veronica didn't think it was ever going to end, until suddenly he thrust into her mouth as far as he could, she cried in agony as she tasted blood from her own mouth and the salty bitter taste of his finish, again causing her to wretch violently. When he let her go he threw her back down to the floor, and she cried. Her voice was hoarse and still all of the emotion in it caused a reaction in myself that was unexpected, I wished I could help her. I wished I could kill him and make it stop. Hunched over herself, her throat swelling and mouth numb. She vomited and choked painfully on the floor as her tears mixed with blood on the ground. And she begged him to stop.

"Please stop."

He used his foot to kick her onto her back and she winced as her spine connected with the concrete. He stood watching her for a few seconds, his eyes gazing over her body as she turned her head to vomit on the ground. He leaned down with his elbows on his knees, and began hoisting her skirt up over her hips as she tried to twist away from him. He yanked her panties down and threw them across the alley, then his fingers caught in the top of her dress pulling it down to reveal her breasts. Her hands covered her face as she sobbed, knowing what would happen next.

He parted her legs roughly and squeezed down between them, slapping her hands away when she tried to fight him off and eventually taking both wrists in one hand and slamming them down above her head, fracturing both wrists in several places. She screamed, and he punched her with his free hand.

She started crying silently to herself, and as his fingers entered her she began to hum softly to herself. The pain unbearable as he pulled, twisted and yanked his fingers inside. Two, then three, until eventually he had his hole hand inside her. She was sore and bleeding by the time he pulled his hand out.

"You wait there I'm not fucking done with you yet, I need a joint." He said, again using a low menacing voice. By now she was just staring at the sky wishing she would die. She knew what was coming next and so do I, and I know I don't want to watch it. But I have no choice, the video in my mind is stuck on play. I feel my mouth making the movements of saying 'no, no' but no sound comes out.

He laughed at her and walked away toward the end of the alleyway towards his car. Her blood boiled, and she felt an overwhelming urge to have her revenge. He has already hurt her and planned worse so in Veronica's mind there was no reason not to fight him. She stood awkwardly, pulling her skirt down and her top up over herself, her blistered feet and bruised and bleeding knee's only making her want to fight more, and she turned to him slowly as he walked away from her. She pounced and brought him down to the ground hard landing on top of him, crying out with anger and fury. The animalistic instinct to fight took over her body and she was no long Veronica, for that short amount of time she was a warrior. A survivor. And I respect her more than any other soul I have ever met for it.

She sat astride him hitting him over and over again not even noticing the pain it caused her hands. When she stopped and looked into the eyes of her monster she had just enough time to spit in his face before the knife connected with the side of her head, I feel a tingle in my left temple telling me that's where it entered her skull killing her straight away, and she fell to the concrete floor.

The wetness on my cheeks tells me just how much the scene I have witnessed affected me, and I notice my body is no longer laid on the ground but curled up in a ball between the bins and concrete wall, shivering and sobbing.

I believe I owe Veronica enough to seek revenge but for now I push all the raw emotion and tears deep down and lock it away. This devil of a man is going to get a surprise when I find him. And I WILL find him.

Chapter 2

My body is no longer tingling and I decide to try stretching. The new muscles feel amazing and it is almost as though they are physically thanking me for the privilege of being used. The rain suddenly appears out of nowhere, showering me in refreshing water as though nature understood I would need cleaning after witnessing such a terrifying scene and I let it wash away my emotion as well as the blood and dirt. I stand and smile at how good I always feel after awakening. After centuries inside nature I can't help but to notice the little pleasures like rubbing my neck and wiggling my toes, although difficult to do in these rather ridiculous red heels. But, I have to admit they do look nice.

I scan the alley way again with my mind as I did when I first awoke, sending out a question and receiving no answer. I know instantly that nature has left me to figure things out on my own. All I know is that if I am awake then there is something going on that must be stopped. Something bad.

I need to figure out what it is threatening the balance and doing so will take help and a safe house. And so, grabbing Veronica's fallen purse and scooping up its contents I begin walking to the end of the alleyway where the option will be simple. Left or right?

I hear voices from the street at the end and slow down hoping to hear more over the clicking of these heels on concrete. There is a couple kissing against a wall, the woman's back pushed roughly against the wall, the man pinning her there making me cringe as they openly display their crude and vulgar need for closeness. More women dressed as scantily clad as Veronica was tonight hover on the corners waving at drivers passing by, a man outside the club with the loud music blaring out onto the street. The man is tall and wide, dressed all in black. He smiles sweetly at me as I walk into view, he must have known Veronica as a regular. He waves me into the club but I walk straight past him leaving him looking confused. I need to be away from people that recognise Veronica right now so I can have a chance to be Violet.

"Bad customer Vera? Hurry back its nearly happy hour!" the blonde yells over the road and I grin awkwardly and walk faster.

I carry on walking down the same street, past shop windows bearing items that hold no interest to me. I am here for a purpose and that purpose has nothing to do with revealing clothes or tattoos and piercings.

People are flooding the streets shouting and fighting, or singing loudly and obnoxiously while falling hysterically to the floor. They walk along the roads, holding up taxi's taking others home or to a different club. Men intoxicated start whistling at me and yelling things like "Eh up love how much you charge for the full job?" and laughing as they attempt to not fall over and I can't help but feel almost intimidated by the leering glances. I continue walking forward, unsure of my destination until I find it I guess, taking in the sights and sounds all around me. The roaring of the cars, the thunderous booms of bottles slamming against walls as men attempt to win the affection of women by vandalising property, the ridiculous chants of drunken people in groups.

AWAKE AGAIN

I stop outside another night club, feeling an undeniable pull towards it. Gold posts with thick red ropes joining them surrounding people cueing to go inside. I see nothing particularly enthralling about the building yet the pull is obvious, I just have to go inside. Two men wearing all black suits and sunglasses stand at the doors waving people through as did the man at the previous club. I join the back of the cue of people and sneak inside with the group in front of me.

The first thing I notice when walking through the doors is a woman sitting at a booth taking peoples coats, giving them numbered tickets in return. It baffles me until one of Veronica's memories sparks and shows me it is to keep a track of peoples coats so they can give them back at the end of the night. I follow a group of people through another door to the right and am instantly met with a wall of music hitting my body, I feel the beat more than I hear it and walk slowly, cautiously, into the room. The blinding lights flashing on and off at an alarming rate causing it to take a moment or two before I can see properly.

I stand with my mouth open in shock, staring at the scene before me. Women are dancing inside clear boxes sticking out of the walls wearing nothing but their underwear and shoes. Three sliver poles are positioned randomly in the building from floor to ceiling with tables and chairs scattered around them and as I watch transfixed women manoeuvre their bodies around the poles in a way I can only describe as sensual art, men sitting and watching them in amazement much like I am now.

Chandeliers dripping with diamonds look exquisite as they hang from the black ceiling, the lights dancing and bouncing around the red shimmery floor adding to the flashy expensive theme of the club. Black tables with large red bean bag type seats are scattered all down one side of the club and in the middle is a large square of raised floor, it looks like thick glass on top of a swimming pool, yet people are standing on it.

"Welcome to Glitterific, the most amazing club in town. Can I get you a drink?" the woman appeared almost out of nowhere in front of her, her black lycra body suit hugging every inch of her torso except the large cleavage escaping the top while the short cut shorts of the suit and black glitter high heels make her legs look long and sleek and elegant. A black pattern entwined up one leg looking as though barbed wire was climbing her body.

"Erm…" I stutter not knowing what was happening.

"Anyone who looks at the dancers the way you did is here for some fun. I'm Sandy, find me if you want a good time." Sandy was extremely attractive and I smile shyly as she walks away winking provocatively, leaving my attention to the club again.

When I look down again I see the people aren't standing on the glass floor, they are dancing on it! Grinding their hips together, practically having sex right there in front of everyone! My mouth almost hits the floor as my eyes widen even more with silent fascination. The girls are hardly wearing any clothes, and I see I fit in nicely wearing Veronicas work clothes. I find the chewing gum in her bag and place it inside my mouth, suddenly needing to feel cleaner after the brutal attack I just sort of witnessed happen to this body. I am reminded of the blood I must be covered in and rush to find a ladies room, thankful for the dim lighting in the club. Pushing past the crowds

AWAKE AGAIN

of people cueing restlessly for a drink I see the hidden doors with a plaque on each, elegant writing shows me the ladies and the gents.

When I enter the ladies I find my reflection in the floor to ceiling mirror to be spotless except a little dirt and blood on my knees. I discover I not only appreciate the heels but getting a good look at this dress shows a beautifully fitted corset top with short skirt matching the colour of the heels. Veronica had good taste. I get to have a good long look at myself while I am here and see these eyes are a hazel brown colour matching the long hair cascading down over my shoulders. I clean myself up a little with the limited provisions I have, brush my teeth and run a comb through my hair trying to look slightly more presentable.

Leaving the smell of the toilets, the sounds of a woman being sick and her friend slurring her words of comfort, I enter the club again and decide to get a close up view of the people dancing.

Standing at the side of the dance floor I feel someone behind me, my senses go into hyper drive and I cast out my mind for assistance getting a mental plan of the room and keeping it just in case. When I turn however, I see a young looking male with a childish grin on his face.

"Buy you a drink?" he asks. I quickly scan Veronica's memory bank for social skills, trying to find how I'm supposed to act or what I'm supposed to say. I'm a vampire, a warrior of the earth for crying out loud and I don't even know how to react to a boy asking to buy me a drink! Jeez that's humiliating!

"Yeah sure, I'll have a vodka and coke." I smile at him after only a brief pause finding a few of Veronica's memories, I bring my legs together and lean all of my weight on one foot, my hips thrust out at one side. This is courting now? It used to be falling in love, asking for your father's permission and proving you are worthy. Now it's buying her a drink? Humans really are going downhill.

"Great, wait here." he runs away to the counter where other people are cueing. The word 'bar' flashing in my mind.

I turn and again find myself fascinated by the dancers, watching mesmerised by the moving and swaying to the sounds of the fast paced music. They aren't very good, but they are smiling and having fun. Letting go of frustration. The care free vibe I get from the entire building is absolutely exhilarating.

"Sorry that took so long, I'm jerry." he says handing me the drink I don't really want. I hadn't even noticed him return. He leads me over to a table next to the dancers as I pretend to sip the disgusting brown liquid.

"Veronica." I reply deciding to give him the name of the body and not the mind.

I sit opposite him and cross one leg over the other, listening as he begins telling me about his college. I don't know what a college is but I attempt to look interested. All I really want to do is dance like the others are. To be human. Jerry tells me he is on his college football team and I lose myself to disinterest with talk of 'off-side' and 'scoring goals'. My gaze drifting from Jerry to the dancers and back again.

My eyes catch someone across the dance floor, he is watching me with a confusing look on his face. I turn and look around to see who else he could be staring at but when my gaze returns his eyes are glued on me with a fiery burn, and I'm not sure why but my breathing speeds up. I find myself noting how attractive he is! Short black hair. Brown eyes like mine, but his seem to have more depth and history than others surrounding us. As though he knows what real pain is. He is wearing a black shirt and dark blue jeans with black shoes, his sleeves rolled up to his elbows showing off the tantalising shape of the muscles in his arms through the thin cotton.

He is sitting with a woman who is hardly wearing any clothes, less than me! A green luminous piece of material stretched so far across her breasts it looks like it would snap off and take someone's eye out, and some very short shorts of a matching colour, blonde hair combed up as high as it would go and dreadful long pink nails to match her lips so obviously made bigger with the use of a lot of make-up. She is talking nonstop much like Jerry beside me and I smile to see he is probably in the same situation I find myself in. My smile widens when I realise the situation is completely normal, the closest I have been too human for at least a millennia. With the clothes Veronica wore tonight I am surprised I haven't had more looks in here. I feel much more comfortable knowing he is probably just sympathising with my situation, although I still can't peel my eyes away from him.

After a minute of me staring off into the crowd Jerry makes his way to stand in front of me, blocking my view as he holds his hand out waiting for me to do something. A momentary panic sets in as I franticly scan Veronica's memory bank for what my next move should be. I gently place my hand in his and let him pull me up to the dance floor. Now THAT I don't mind. I have been desperate since walking in the door to be a part of them, not caring and just moving for a little while. I am aware of the nagging at the back of my mind telling me I shouldn't be here but I can't help the overwhelming need to get on the dance floor.

And so there I am, taking a moment to scan the people around me and copy their movements. My hips swaying, bringing my arms above my head, moving my feet to a very over powering beat from somewhere high above me when suddenly Jerry is holding my hips against his, and rubbing his groin against my behind. This I don't like at all. I step away quickly giving him the evil eyes, but he just laughs and continues grabbing my waist trying to bring me back to him again.

I push him away softly, completely aware that if I unleash my full powers on him he wouldn't survive it, and I do everything within my power to keep control of the situation by taking a few steps away from him, hoping to lose him in the sea of dancers. When I turn back I see him holding his hands up in defeat laughing and dancing on his own.

I turn away and join the crowd, allowing the rhythm to enter my body as it begins to move on its own, my arms snaking up above my head with the thunderous roar from above taking control of my body and becoming part of me as I forget everyone and everything around me and just dance like I haven't a care in the world.

When I open my eyes I see the man that was staring at me through the dancers, standing right in front of me and staring behind me with nothing but evil intent. I turn slowly to see Jerry about to lift my skirt in a very childish attempt to win back glory in front of his friends I notice cheering him on from the edge.

"I believe the lady told you to fuck off!" he doesn't need to shout over the booming music to be heard, his voices carries easily.

"Who the fuck are you man?"

The mystery man doesn't answer, he just takes a step forward and seemingly shoves him lightly, yet jerry is flung backwards from the dance floor and within a matter of seconds escorted out of the building. The man who came to my rescue, all be it unnecessarily, turns towards me.

I catch the breath this body is so adamant on me taking and again my heart is hammering inside me *'what the hell?'* He looks confused as though he doesn't even know why he did that, mirroring my very thoughts with a single furrow of his brow.

"Cole." he says smoothly, his voice like a blanket on my skin easing away any discomfort. I tingle; but not in the same way the change made me tingle. This is different, as though my body is expecting something more.

"Veronica." I feel instantly fraudulent giving him the wrong name where moments before I had given it so easily to jerry, and he takes my hands, placing them on his shoulders as his find their way to my hips. He keeps his body a good way from mine and there is most definatly no grinding involved with his swaying!

This is nice, this is respectful. As though he is as old as I am. We don't even feel the need to talk to each other. He sways and turns and somehow manages to make this old fashioned taste full dance fit the new fast beat music. His eyes scan my face as I try to make sense of what is happening with the very limited experience I have, his brow still creased with curiosity. My lips part, and I can't take my eyes from his. We dance like this until the music changes, then he moves me to the edge of the dance floor where it isn't as crowded so we can dance and talk.

"So Veronica, I haven't seen you around."

"I'm new in town." well... it's not a complete lie!

"I see, staying with family?" he smiles, soothing away all of my worries and concerns and making me melt under his warm watch full eyes. He brings his face closer to mine as though trying to smell me, the warmth radiating from him as his face is inches from my neck making me shiver with delight when his breath gently caresses my skin.

"Sort of." My voice shakes a little and cracks. I start to get nervous again but I can't understand why.

"Well Veronica I think we might have to arrange another meeting sometime, I must say I am quite interested in learning more about you."

"I'm afraid I'm rather busy." I whimper, everything going numb. I feel my tongue fumbling in my mouth trying to find the words.

"You had time to come in here tonight." He accuses confidently with a smile so radiant I stare at his lips and almost beg him to kiss me.

"I don't know why I came here tonight, I don't usually do things like this." And again I am telling the truth although not as much as I want to. I want to confess everything to this man I don't even know.

"Well I'm pleased you did Veronica. Very pleased indeed." he says in my ear as we dance cheek to cheek.

Warm breath tickles my earlobe and it sends shivers down my spine, which surprise me so much my knees buckle and I start to fall. Luckily Cole is holding me by my hips and catches me with his hands around my waist, to all of the other dancers it just looks like part of the dance.

Before I know it his mouth is on mine and I don't know if it was him or me that made it happen, all I know is everything I have ever known has been thrown out of the window. Nothing matters except this very kiss. It makes me feel both happy to be awake and here at this moment in time and sad that I can never tell him the truth about myself all at the same time. My toes curl in anticipation but I don't even know what I anticipate! Here I am, a warrior weak at the knees. Literally! All over a man.

His hands tighten around my waist and pull me closer to him with a desperation I feel flooding from him and entering my own body. But this is so different to how Jerry held me moments ago, Jerry did it out of selfish want for a woman whereas what Cole is doing now is pure lust for me.

I feel his arousal against my hip and a whole new sensation takes over me, feelings I have never felt before and never even dreamt I would feel are bursting from me. I grab his hair and hold him to me tighter. I can't explain what is going on. Even my fingertips are feeling electric! His tongue enters my mouth exploring me, devouring me in a way so intimate that a sound escapes my throat. It feels divine, causing me to shudder and ideas to alight in my head!

There is no music, no people, no bar, nothing. He doesn't even taste of alcohol as I had expected. The entire encounter is simply amazing. His hands are on my back with an urgency mirroring my own, one hand going slowly down towards my behind.

Someone pushes against me and I break contact on instant alert for danger. By the time I turn back to Cole he is gone. I stand alone on the dance floor cursing myself for the disappointment I feel welling up inside of me, and for letting myself get so caught up.

The whole time I am telling myself off I am also aware of the one thing that has surprised me more than anything so far, the encounter with Cole had me feeling human. I have no idea what that means or what I am supposed to do with the information. A girlish smile plays on my lips as I think maybe he is my soul mate. But I quickly rid myself of such nonsense, those are the thoughts of humans. I am a vampire, I don't have a soul mate. I barely have a soul.

Chapter 3

I take a moment to compose myself in the crisp night air outside of the club and analyse what I know so far. For starters I know that if I am awake then I am here for a very important reason, a dangerous one at that. I know that the others shall be waking very soon and start looking for me, and since I am always the first to awaken it is usually down to me to sort out a safe place to hide out while we gather our thoughts and information. Usually, vampires like to work alone with nobody to slow them down. I and a few others however have bonded for reasons we aren't entirely sure about yet, which means we can sense and track each other when necessary. We gather shortly after our bodies are finished with the transformation and we work together to hunt and destroy.

I cast out my mind in hope of reaching some old friends that may have been reincarnated into this strange and frightening time, and I find myself almost scared when I find no one close by. In all the times I have awoken, even before bonding with the others, I have never felt as alone and vulnerable as I do standing on the path outside club glitter with nowhere to go and not an idea of what I am supposed to do. I decide to walk to keep my body busy and hopefully not draw too much attention to myself and my mind starts thinking about my friends, and how much I miss them right now.

George is a good soul with a very slight rebellious streak that just makes him adorable, we picked him up during his first awakening. He was so confused, we knew instantly he was meant to be with us. When the first awakening happens nature gives us the what but not the why, so he knew he was looking for a threat that he had to defeat but he didn't understand why he was looking for it. We spent a short time filling him in on what he was now and in all honesty we all took a shine to him straight away, except Brian. He saw another male in the group as a threat to himself for some reason.

Brian I can't explain, he is with us simply because he wanted to be, and so we welcomed him. He has never contributed anything to the group or even fit in really but he stays with us because he wants to. I find him tedious at times and have on more than one occasion had to fend him off and tell him rather forcefully I have no interest in him what so ever. Yet he always seems to think I am merely playing hard to get. The truth is I have never had any interest in anyone! Until now I mean.

Clara and Damien are soul mates, even though vampires don't really have soul mates. The two will stumble across each other before finding us and will turn up here together. Every time they awake they somehow manage to fall in love all over again even though they look different every single time. Vampires normally have sex don't get me wrong, they find a partner be it human or warrior that they can connect with and they enjoy being intimate. But it is just sex. No vampire to my knowledge has ever been able to keep a relationship yet these two have managed to remain happy together for centuries. They fight with each other, for each other. There love is so pure it is astonishing. They are a perfect match and perfect for our little group, their differences of opinions are easily settled by both simply listening to the other and thinking of things from their perspective. That quality is getting harder and harder to find as time goes on.

We all work together finding the threat and destroying it, sometimes another vampire gets there before we do and we all go back within nature, sometimes others will join us for a short period of time to help with finding or defeating the threat but most don't wish to bond. They find the ties too emotional. Brian is the only vampire I know of who seems to get jealous of others. Barring myself, there is no one better, we excel in different areas, having a specific quality about us that in fact is linked directly with our purpose, or that's how the rest of us like to think of it anyway. We have yet to find our purposes but with every awakening we succumb to the idea that maybe we don't have one any more.

I walk, noticing again the goofy smile on my face as I get to thinking about handsome strangers, and this time I allow the mild distraction to consume my thoughts. Heck, a girl is allowed to think of her first kiss a few times isn't she? I get to thinking why I have never searched for love before, something has always been in my mind telling me it's not important and I am only now beginning to question whether or not I didn't think it was important or if I was I just afraid. I wonder for a moment if my encounter with Cole has made me want to search for someone to be intimate with, but still the idea doesn't appeal to me.

When I think of being intimate with Cole however I feel the same tensions in my stomach as I felt earlier, it must be a reaction to Cole. Maybe he is my soul mate. Again I swoon like a thirteen year old girl for a minute or two before crushing my own dreams with harsh reality. I do not have a soul mate, of course my first kiss was amazing it was my first kiss, I have nothing to compare it to. I grow angry with myself remembering I am a vampire and here to defeat the threat of the world's balance yet for a moment I almost started thinking about marriage and true love. After ridding myself of such childish silly thoughts I feel a pull and again cast out my senses to the spirits surrounding me, finding an old friend living not too far away.

I look at the buildings surrounding me and think of how drastically the world has changed in the time I was asleep, I call it asleep but it's not like I lay down and just snooze for a few centuries as your legends would have you believe, the very idea of it is just preposterous! When we aren't needed our souls live within nature, helping the trees to grow and winds to blow. Our energy is used to keep the world alive until such a time as we need it again, during which our energy; or soul if you prefer, is thrust into the body of a person who's soul has just departed yet when it happens we are thrust into a new world every time. Obviously I have all of Veronica's memories so it's easier to understand the strangeness that surrounds me but I am still amazed at how the streets have changed and how people have become worryingly lazy, almost completely dependent on technology for everything from organising a schedule to making a simple cup of coffee.

After a very short walk I find myself outside a building that I sense belongs to Alliyana, and I anxiously knock on the door taking note of the flowers in her garden and how simple and cute this little area is in which she lives. The smile on my face spreads even further when I see the light flicker on behind the door, the excitement having me giggling before she opens it! When she does open the door I see the uneasiness in her eyes as she somehow recognises me but isn't overly sure how or where from.

"Ever kiss a vampire prince?" I lean down and whisper in her ear. My soul has reached out to her, which has brought her own ancient soul forwards, but my words remind her of who I am.

Alliyana is the reincarnated soul of an ancient 'Mermaid', trapped within the body of a mortal as her sacrifice to capture a fire demon within the ocean and imprison him forever. As long as mermaids walk on land he remains trapped under water.

I giggle with excitement as I see the memories flood back into her mind. She looks at me again with new eyes and I can feel her senses reaching out to me, the twinkle in the smile she gives that reaches from ear to ear is beautiful.

"Violet." she whispers and grabs me, pulling me towards her in a strong encompassing hug while wailing her excitement to the rest of the street and pulling me inside her home. Her bright red hair flailing behind her tall skinny frame as she seems to float on air down the hallway into a large open plan kitchen diner.

As she puts the kettle on and makes herself a coffee, not asking me since she knows I don't eat or drink anything, I tell her all about Veronica and the memories I witnessed.

"Honestly Violet you wouldn't believe what happens in the world today. It's enough what happened to poor Veronica to make my stomach turn and yet worse is happening right now as we speak and there is nothing we can do about it anymore. Things are not how they used to be, people are cruel and vindictive, and they prefer to keep themselves to themselves. If you try to help someone chances are you will be deemed worse than the problem your trying to help with!" she is ranting about society and I can't help but let her continue, listening. Intrigued by her words.

"And if you think that's bad you should see the way they treat the people they do like, always commenting behind backs and spreading rumours, all it takes is for one person to be late home from a shopping trip and before you know it an entire town is talking about a made up affair! And can you believe all the magic is gone? You would be very lucky to find any sacred ground on this earth anymore humans have destroyed it all with their new technology and high buildings, always trying to make everything newer and shinier. That's if they are doing anything at all some of them sit on their backsides in front of the television all day long eating terrible food and either complaining they are putting on too much weight and the government aren't doing enough to help them or their television isn't big enough and it's the governments fault! And don't even get me started on this whole 'size 0' thing, the way some of the girls today behave would turn your stomach. Some as young as ten years old wearing hardly any clothes, throwing up their dinners to lose weight and dreaming of the perfect man."

"Well if the dancing is anything to go off I can already tell the human race is doomed soon enough." I answer without even thinking after being so caught up with Alliyana's rant.

"Wait, who said anything about dancing?" She looks at me confused. *Fuck.* A slight slip of the tongue that I can't get out of.

"Oh, I went into a club. You know, to see what

it was like." I shrug, knowing had I been human my face would be beetroot red.

"A club? You mean like a night club? Like.... really?"

"Yes a night club, is there a problem with that?" I snap at her, but she just giggles back at me.

"Well yeah! So you're emotional over Veronica's death, curious about a night club and sensitive about someone asking questions? I think this might be the most human I have ever seen you." she smiles at me sweetly ignoring the sharp look, but when she mentions me being human it reminds me of Cole and feeling more human. I fidget with my fingertips on the counter in front of me.

"Now what?" she asks matter of factly.

"Nothing!" I say trying to act surprised that she thought something was wrong, but her face doesn't change at all as she stares at me waiting for an explanation. I huff and slump my shoulders knowing she isn't about to let the subject go.

"Alliyana...."

"Call me Ally."

"Ally. I met someone." I say simply. And she just nods her head for me to continue, eyes widening. "In the club, I met a guy called Jerry who bought me a drink, talked non-stop about college and football and then asked me to dance. Watching the dancers was amazing, how care free they were and how they moved so confidently it was breath taking even if they were terrible at it and physically sickening with far too much gyrating. But being up there was kind of frightening, he was grinding and grabbing and all forceful. I nearly lost it! But then Cole was standing there, he had been watching me through the dancers earlier, and he pushed Jerry away and sort of took over. He was all swaying and swooning and moving delicately. I could have sworn he was an old soul yet I couldn't sense him at all. And when we kissed it was like he was taking me to another world, one with no people or dance floors or anything just the two of us. It was like ….. Magic." I focus my stare on the kitchen work top and think about how nothing mattered except that kiss until Alliyana starts talking to me again.

"Hair colour?"
"Black."
"Eyes?"
"Brown."
"Good looking?"
"Extremely."
"Single?"
"Huh?"
"These days you have to be very careful, he could already be married."

"He didn't act like a married man." I say, although I don't actually know why I am defending him against a question I don't know the answer to.

"The married one's never do." she replies a little bitter.

"Oh!" Romance these days seems like a roller coaster! First of all I find the art of wooing a female is right out the window but now I find that once he has one he isn't satisfied and needs more!

"So he was human?" she asks confused.
"Yes, why?"
"I just can't think why nature would give you a human soul mate, what with you being a vampire and all. It just doesn't make sense." her brows are creased and she goes back to sipping her coffee.

"He is not my soul mate! Ally, I don't have a

soul mate, I am far too busy for anything like that." I shake my head and throw my hands up in frustration, but she just laughs at me.

"Yeah cos what you described happens to everyone when they kiss!" Her words are sarcastic and it makes me think what I felt wasn't a normal kiss. Maybe he is my soul mate, maybe he has something to do with why we are here, and maybe he has something to do with my purpose!

"And what about you? Found love yet in this life time?" I nudge her elbow smiling, both curious and eager to change the topic of conversation.

"Violet, a lady does not kiss and tell!" she says and sits up straight mocking me.

"Your right, a lady most certainly does not kiss and tell. However you are no lady, you are a mermaid, saviour of the entire planet. You sacrificed your way of life for the soul of every person and being. That is not the act of a lady. Oh yes and there was that fling with that vampire prince if you recall before you turned into a goddess. When you were both betrothed? Where is Demetre?" She almost spurts coffee out of her nose as I recall out loud her little adventure with love.

"There is a man in my life yes." And she tries really hard to hide the smile but fails so badly I can't help but laugh. Her cheeks turning the brightest red colour I have seen! "His name is Dave and he is away on business for another week or so. He lives a few miles down the road, but I am thinking of having him move in with me. And yes, our souls seem to connect before you ask." The smile grows more and more secretive as it stretches from ear to ear.

"Anyway I'm going up to bed, I have an early swimming session booked for the morning."

"Swimming session?" I arch my brows.

"Yes. I'm an Olympic swimmer." She winks laughing. "Feel free to use the house as much as you need to, there is a spare key inside a false rock outside if you sense for it you will find it. You think about lover boy, watch some television, read a book I don't care but as you know I need my sleep. Goodnight." She puts her cup in the sink and walks out of the room, I hear her footsteps going up the creaky stairs and I walk around the kitchen exploring a little, thinking of the possibilities that I could perhaps meet Cole again before my mission is over.

Chapter 4

"George! At last!" I scold him playfully and he walks inside, looking mystified around the strange home with pictures hanging on walls and fancy patterns covering the floor.

"So the house is...?"

"I have awoken Alliyana, she is letting us use her home as a safe house, and has offered assistance if needed." I smile at him to relax and he shrugs out of the black leather coat he was wearing, placing it over the back of one of the chairs at the breakfast bar leaving him standing in black jeans and t-shirt. His messy ginger hair framing his green eyes.

"Wow the mermaid is awake?" I nod as he wanders from one side of the breakfast bar to the other clearly trying to work out what it is for.

George's soul has a 'thing' for Alliyana's soul. It isn't love or even attraction. It is more like... adoration. He looks on her as though she is a goddess. Which makes sense since she technically was, he listens attentively to all of her tales. He spends a little time wandering around the kitchen and playing with the television on the counter top for a short while. When he spots the microwave I see a look of concentration cross his face as he scans the memories of his body's previous owner, but get a little confused when he recoils in horror.

"Women don't cook anymore?" he actually looks afraid and I can't figure out why since he doesn't eat any more!

"Women work now George, they don't have the time to cook. They buy the food readymade and heat it up in this." I point to the microwave but George continues looking almost offended. "The worst thing about it George is that some women DO call that cooking!" His eyes widen even more and he turns away shaking his head, moving from room to room inspecting everything from light switches to the flushing toilet under the stairs.

We settle in the living room with the television on while we await the others. Clara and Damien arrive while we search the channels to find something interesting to watch.

"Hello." I say as I open the door to them both holding hands. "Come inside, the house is Alliyana's and she has no idea what the threat could be about so I will just let you two dive straight into exploring electricity as we have done and I will meet you in the television room." I turn away after smiling and letting them in, to go back and watch television. What can I say, I'm hooked!

I hear them in the kitchen having almost exactly the same discussion me and George had about the microwave, although Clara is much more interested in the vacuum cleaner. Eventually they meet us in the television room and also become mesmerised by the flashing screen. We remain sitting there mesmerised until Brian arrives.

We all hear the knock on the door and stand to organise ourselves. Now we are all here, no more slacking. Straight to business. Damien opens the door to Brian as the rest of us gather in the kitchen and prepare ourselves.

"So why are we here then?" Brian is straight into asking questions as we knew he would be.

"We do not know yet Brian we were waiting for you, as we do every awakening." Clara says as though it was obvious, which in her defence it kind of was.

"OK so let's go and find out then." he stands as though to leave and we are all staring at him in shock.

"Whoa, Calm down there Brian let's make a plan first shall we. You know like we always do." He sighs and sits back down mumbling *you mean wait for our orders!* Under his breath. "Well I suggest we wake some more old souls, I am not feeling any magical changes in the atmosphere so I'm guessing whatever the threat is it isn't major just yet. We need to go out there and wake old souls and find out if they know anything that is going on."

"So now I can go?" asks Brian coldly and I nod, he stands and walks out of the house. We all look at each other with mild disbelief, he is always arrogant but never before have we known him this bad.

"OK that was weird, so anyway I say we go awaken old souls to help us find the threat. They are always at the back of the mind but they pick up on this kind of thing so get sensing and get searching people. I will go alone, as will George, Clara and Damien can go together obviously and Brian can go on his own. Since he has already done." We all walk out of the door together sending out our senses for old souls. I sense a few nearby.

I decide to head for the closest soul I sense and before long find my train of thoughts returning to Cole and how I kissed him. Or he kissed me. Or whatever. You know. I fell and my lips kind of landed on his. Whatever happened it sure was unbelievable, I can feel my body responding just to thoughts of him!

Thoughts of Cole cloud my concentration and I struggle to focus on finding the soul I need, it is as though I am intoxicated with him and he is numbing my senses. I am almost stumbling over my own feet as I walk!

Something definitely grabs my interest as I turn onto a street corner. This is the street I need to be on, and in one of the driveways I see a car looking rather familiar. A dark red banger of a car with the license plate reading 3IG D1K is parked in the first drive way, next door to the house I need to be at. This should be interesting!

I knock on the door of the house with the old soul and I feel Kirsty's soul is strong, so it might not be too difficult to waken her at least. Kirsty's soul is that of what you would call a Banshee, although again I see the legend has become a little altered since magical creatures roamed. A banshee would protect her family, she was a creature of magnificent knowledge. In your legends now it is believed a banshee would merely wail at the death of a family member whether she knew about them passing or not, but there is no detail in to why she would wail. A banshee could feel her family much the same way I feel my friends through our bond. She would feel the loss as though losing an arm and she would rip anyone apart to save her own.

But they were by far good creatures, balanced mostly but if they did tip more to one side it was always the side of evil. They wouldn't protect another's child, or feed the hungry with their spares. They never did anything particularly wrong, unless you got on the wrong side of them. Thankfully this particular banshee owes me since I rescued one of her babies during one my first awakenings.

Kirsty opens the door and again I see vague recollection gather on her face as she sort of recognises me. Much the same as Alliyana had although Kirsty also had a slight malicious feel to her at the same time. Yep, this is definatly the soul of a banshee!

"What do you want?" she asks confused and I send out my soul to bring hers forward, and yet again I watch as her face goes from confusion to understanding, and finally to relief.

"Hi Kirsty, how's it going?" I ask and she smiles ever so slightly at me, standing aside to let me in her home.

"Hey Violet, things aren't too bad. Obviously there's a lot worse going on in the world I don't know about or you wouldn't be here. What's it this time?" You can tell a banshee soul straight away from the attitude in which they speak. Straight to the point, no silliness or unwanted chatter.

"I was kind of hoping you could tell me!" I say answering her question and knowing my own by the furrow of her brow. "Great you don't know anything." she points to her living room where she rudely leaves the television on while we talk, although I didn't expect anything else from her.

"I haven't heard of anything, take it you guys haven't been awake long yet then. Well I'll do my best to spread the word and get back to you but I can't wake souls like you can."

"That would be great thank you Kirsty, it's not much but right now we will take whatever help we can get. Got to think positive and all that jazz!" I say and she just smiles at me.

"Hey before I go what do you know about the man next door?" she looks surprised by my question but answers anyway.

"Who, James? Well he keeps himself to himself just as I like the neighbours to. Why?"

"He abused the girl that had this body, killed her soon after."

"Why do you care?" She asks the question seriously. Kirsty is naturally programmed to protect her family with whatever needs doing, she has so much power and strength and love for her own inside her that there isn't a lot of room left for compassion. It's not her fault, it is simply how she was made.

"I care because I can." She nods appreciatively. The discussion isn't heated at all she was genuinely curious. But my answer means more to her since I know the truth is she wishes she *could* care more.

"Well he is a bit of a twat really, I don't get along with any of my neighbours. Too loud! A bit scruffy, very deep in the drug business. Lives with a lass but I think he roughs her up, none of my business though." She leaves it there, not much but enough.

"Thank you Kirsty, remember if you hear or feel anything send for us." I turn and walk out without waiting for her to show me out, knowing she won't want a hug or anything, and guessing she already knows why I'm using her back door. I jump over the wall outside into the back garden of the house next door. There are no lights on in the house as I try the broken wooden door and find it held closed from the inside with rope as the handle has clearly been broken off.

I close the door, or I try too, silently behind me and walk through the kitchen into the living room, where there is a large body laid on the sofa covered in an old torn up coat. It is moving ever so slightly and turns to look at the doorway where I stand.

"Baby you came back!" he says and sure enough the voice is very much familiar. He staggers and stands up, but falls back down straight away. It is still dark in the room, so all he can see is a figure in the door way. "I'm sorry baby you know you piss me off when you do that, you were asking for it you know you were. You shouldn't piss me off like that." I stay silent and let him carry on slurring, which seems to infuriate him. "Don't fucking ignore me baby cos I'll give you another fucking black eye on the other side of your face! You can't be angry at me you silly cow, you were the one fucking talking to him again. I know he is your brother but you know he doesn't fucking like me. I told you to stop talking to him and I find out you been meeting him? Of course I was fucking angry. Ain't you even gonna say sorry?" he is mumbling his words worse than he did in the alley way, the smell of whiskey infused with that of the weed I assume he has been taking. Just as he is about to carry on talking the front door opens and a light flicks on, a small woman with dark hair, green eyes and a black bruise covering her cheek stands looking at me confused.

James stands straight away looking at her, then to me. Now he can see me with the lights on, and I lean against the door way and stare back at him casually.

"What the fuck are you doing here?" he yells, slightly sobered for seeing me.

"You called for me baby, said you want a good time. Said you would pay full price this time." he stares at me confused, going from me to the woman who closes the front door and walks further into the room.

"James, what is going on?" she asks him after looking at me still wearing Veronicas work clothes.

"You can't be here, it's impossible. You can't fucking be here." his words are shaky and he sits back down, mouth wide open in shock.

"Hey don't let me ruin the party, I can wait." I take a seat on the chair facing James while he sits on the sofa staring at me.

"How? What do you want? How did you find me?" he is nervous, I can tell by his white face and shaking hands. But heck, wouldn't you be nervous if the person you abused and killed turned up at your house.

"Why James it's almost as though you aren't pleased to see me. We don't want your friend here to think I did something bad now, would we?" I allow a little viciousness to make its way into my voice as I lean forward, hands resting gently on my knees. I instantly regret my actions when the poor woman seems a little frightened of me.

"What is going on?"

"Go ahead James, you tell her exactly what is going on." I sit back again and inspect the fingernails of my right hand as though bored.

"I.... I don't.... It can't be.... this is impossible!" his eyes are wide and his hands run through his hair, words jumbled as he mumbles some kind of pathetic response that just pisses me off even more. Just sitting here with him is reminding me of what he did, the entire scene flashing before my mind again. I sit forward yet again and this time my voice is dripping with as much evil as there is in my eyes. And it makes him whimper slightly, like a cornered animal.

"I am here to find justice."

"What do you want?" he asks seriously.

"Justice."

"And how much does justice cost? I have money and drugs, what do you want?"

"Oh James, there is no drug on the planet that

could affect me and as for money I have no need." he looks confused and slightly afraid. I bask in the feeling of being in control, knowing I could lose control of myself at any minute. "I do not live anywhere so don't require furniture, I cannot have babies so no dependent children, I do not have an addiction. I have nothing to lose, *baby*."

"The money is in the kitchen, it's all yours. In the biscuit tin. Take it. There's a lot, everyone wants things you're stupid if you don't." he is begging and I just continue to laugh at him.

"What is going on?" Asks the voice from the corner.

"Amy shut the fuck up and let me handle this!" he hisses at her and my gaze turns straight back to him as I feel something inside me almost howl with anger. I can't help myself from leaning forward and slapping his face for daring to speak to a woman with such disrespect in front of me.

"She can talk to whomever she wishes to talk to, if she wants to ask my opinion on the fucking weather she can. Understand?" He nods as my voice raises in anger, a trail of blood running down from his mouth. "She has more right to speak to me than you do! You do not speak to anyone like that you have no right. For the rest of this conversation you speak only when spoken to do you understand James?" He cowers slightly and I turn back to Amy. "You are the one he 'taught a lesson' to then, before he beat, abused and murdered Veronica." She gasps, not realising the extent of his actions until now. "I'm sorry for frightening you, you have nothing to fear from me."

"Murdered?" she whispers to me.

"No fucking way, I thought I did but I can't have, you are sitting right there we can both see you.

Baby this *is* the fucking prostitute see I ain't no killer!"

"No James, I am something else." his face falls yet again and he stares at me with confusion in his eyes. And just as I was expecting he leaps across the room at me, his hands finding my throat easily since I don't bother putting up a fight. Amy is screaming and backing away against a wall, I see the worry on her face and know she sees the monster he really is even if she couldn't see it before. After a moment he releases his hands finding that there was actually no struggle. I didn't fight, I didn't gasp for breath, in fact my face should be turning red and yet I merely sit staring at him without breathing or making a sound. I check my nails out bored again and he backs off slowly, terrified.

"Fuck this." he says and pushes Amy over on his way out of the door. I jump up and help Amy, who stares from me to the door.

"You have nothing to fear Amy as I said, I am here for James. Are you OK?" I ask and she nods, checking her body for any cuts or bruises that weren't already there.

"I think so." she breaths at me. I help her to the sofa where she sits and watches me walk into the kitchen. I turn the light on and get her a glass of water. I grab the money James told me about and walk back into the living room.

"Do you have family you can stay with?" I ask and she nods again, she has had a major shock. I hold the money out so she can see.

"I'm taking this for people that need it, you go to your family and change your life." And with that I walk out of the house. When I turn and look back I see Amy at the window watching me walk away, a look of empowerment on her face and I hope she listens to my advice and leaves while she can.

I walk out of the gate at the end of the garden and start following James, he is unfit and I am a vampire. It doesn't take me long to catch up with him. I stop running when I get beside him.

"Where are we going?" I ask casually, as though we could be on our way to the cinema or something. He just screams and starts running faster in a different direction, and I give him a few moments before catching up with him again. "Are you avoiding me?" I ask innocently, mock offence on my face. He recoils and turns again, running back in the other direction again. "You know, I am starting to think you are trying to run away from me. I don't like that." I grab his arm and pull him. "I know a great place we can go." and I lead him back to the alleyway in which he left Veronica for dead. When we get there I throw him down to the floor and stand watching him clamber up on his knees and cry.

"Please, please don't hurt me. I'll do anything you want. I can get you drugs, I have money, and back at my house there is a stash of money in the kitchen. It's yours take it. It's in the biscuit tin. The drugs are in the bathroom, take the lid off the toilet box and it's a little bag taped inside. A few grand's worth in there take it all. Please just take it all." he is begging me to leave him alone and yet I remember Veronica's experience, and how brave she was compared to him and it fires her up even more. "Sexual favours? Whatever you want. I don't care just please don't kill me." He sits up on his knees begging me and I kick him back to the ground.

"Sexual favours? You are really suggesting sexual favours?" I walk around him. "I am here to teach you a lesson, to show you that what you did to Veronica will not happen again to anyone else by you. And you try bribing me with money, drugs and sex? Do you really think these are things I am interested in?" he closes his eyes knowing he has nothing else to offer.

I lean my heel on his kneecap. He deserves agony for his crimes. I put my foot down with only slight force, but still he screams in pain. The crunching sound telling me I succeeded in breaking his knee and a grin spreads maliciously across my face. I lean down and grab his hair the same way he had held Veronicas when he attacked her, and I look deep into his eyes hoping for any sort of remorse. All I see is fear for himself, not an ounce of sorrow for what he did.

"Having fun?" I ask and he shakes his head with his face screwed up tightly against the pain, the stench of fear oozes from him and I can't help myself but to take pride in my accomplishment, having this evil scumbag whimpering after everything he has done is empowering. "You are not going to abuse any one ever again. And I mean, EVER. Isn't that right James? You are never going to have sex again when I'm through with you." He squeals and starts begging again.

"What are you?" he cries.

"A vampire."

"Are you going to kill me?" The edge of terror in his voice feeds my soul. My only reply is a snarl, like a wild animal about to devour it's pray. I lean my head close to his neck as I let my nails sink into the skin of his scalp, he can barely breathe he is so petrified. I sink my teeth into the clammy flesh and let the blood pour out around my mouth, not for food

AWAKE AGAIN

as humans these days believe. This is how we make our mark. This is how we imprint, bond even. Now whenever this monstrosity even thinks of hurting a woman he will remember me. He will remember this night.

"Please, please leave me alone. Please don't kill me, please leave me alone. I'm sorry I won't do it again. I'm sorry." Repeating his words over and over again between tormented screams of pain. I push his head down to the floor when I am done, his nose shattering on the concrete.

His yelp of pain bounces from one empty surface to another, echoing through the alleyway, and remains unheard over the music of the club on the street just as Veronica's screams had. The memories of Veronicas attack fog my mind and I end this whole encounter, kicking him once in the dick which he dared to force on another human being in such a foul and disgraceful way. The kick sends his entire body forward, scraping his face across the concrete floor. He is frozen in pain for a moment before shifting to hold his extremely injured penis and breathing out very slowly through his teeth, and from the look on his face I know he will never be able to use it again. I lift him by his hair and stare straight into his face.

"If I remember correctly you wanted it *sucked and fucked.* Well I think it's pretty fucked now." With that I throw him back to the ground, his face landing in the pile of blood and vomit still there from Veronica. It seemed fitting that I leave him in exactly the same place, bruised and bloodied. He most definitely won't be abusing anybody ever again. I would be surprised if he walked ever again.

I smile knowing justice has been brought for the abuse Veronica experienced before her death, but now it's time to sort something else out for her.

Chapter 5

I find Veronicas flat by using her memories and nerves take hold of me. What if one of her flat mates come home, how do I handle the situation without leaving them suspicious? Although I soon find my nerves were unwarranted, the whole time I was there I was completely alone. Nobody disturbed me at all as I searched for more appropriate clothing. The flat was a mess, dirty pots everywhere, empty food wrappers littered the floor and a rotten stench hanging in the air making me cover my sensitive nose with my hand. Ash trays piled high with cigarette butts and glasses with lipstick marks still sit on the coffee table. I find Veronica's bedroom, the white door with the hole in the bottom boarded up from the inside, and am instantly surprised to see how tidy and organised everything is. There is a dresser next to her bed with photos of her ex-husband and their son, scented candles scattered all around the room. This woman really was desperate.

Her bed is made to perfection, even the top right corner folded over to allow easier access without ruffling the pink floral sheets, her clothes all neatly folded away in the drawers. No jewellery or ornaments at all and I get the feeling she didn't trust the other girls enough to keep anything valuable here.

After searching through her wardrobe for what seemed like hours I settle on jeans and a pretty black top covered in sequins found right at the back.

I find some flat boots under her bed which seem like the most sensible out of her shoe collection. As I leave the flat I have an image in my head of the way vampires are depicted today, and I laugh to myself at the idea of wearing tight PVC cat suits and high heels while battling some of the demons I have faced.

With my hair brushed and tied back, and all traces of makeup removed I feel much better. Right now there is another task to take care of. I leave the flat with a heavy heart knowing this is going to be very emotional for me seeing as I seem to be feeling all of Veronicas emotions intensified. Who knows, maybe this is my purpose. Maybe it has nothing to do with Cole and the only reason I felt so drawn to him was because I was projecting Veronica's emotions instead of my own. Maybe where I'm headed now and what I'm going to do when I get there is my purpose.

I knock on the door of the house with the green window shutters from Veronica's memory, aware of how early it is but not surprised when her husband, Kane, answers so quickly.

"Can I come in?" I ask quietly, and he stands aside. I see the love in his eyes and the hope that Veronica is home to stay. It warms my lonely heart to know he does love Veronica very much.

I walk in to a sitting room and lean against the door way, looking at the elegantly decorated space and seeing an image flash in my mind of him playfully covering Veronica in paint, white sheets protecting the furniture, Veronica's stomach round and swollen.

"What's the problem?" he asks curious as to what his ex-wife is doing here at this time and I can't think of anything to say. I just hand over the money from James's biscuit tin. His eyes go wide and he looks back up at me.

"Where did you get all of this?" he asks with a

look of dread.

"Is it enough for school?" I breath calmly, overwhelmed by the feelings from Veronica's subconscious reaching out to him.

"That and more!" He breathes. "Veronica this is enough money to put him through University! Where did you get all of this? You're not doing anything illegal are you?"

"You don't need to know where it's from you just need to pay for school. Look after our son and tell him I will always love him." I say lovingly, briefly touching his arm and kissing him on the cheek before turning away from him and walk towards the door.

"Sell everything. My jewellery, clothes, everything. I won't be needing it any more, my only wish is for you two to be OK" I know it's true, I almost feel her with me at that moment thanking me.

"Veronica what is going on!" he demands and I just continue walking away with my head bent, silent tears cascading down my face, amazed at how strong their feelings are for each other, he follows me with tears filling his eyes, reminding me of the scene in her memory of the first time she walked out. I find myself thinking about Cole. Before I do anything else I want to look around and have some time alone with my thoughts.

I decide to walk in the direction I smell water. There's nothing more thought inspiring than flowing water, I have found in every awakening my thoughts are clearer when I find a stream or a river.

The buildings I pass as I walk are very tall, some have glass walls letting you see everything that people are doing inside, and some have balconies where groups of people gather laughing and drinking.

The concrete squares I walk on are jutting out at

all angles. The cars on the roads baffle me. The speed seems unnecessary and greedy. I continue following the scent of water hoping to find it soon and sure enough I round a corner, veering away from the busy streets and bustling noises, and am met with a fantastic view.

    I climb the grassy hill in front of me and stand on the river bank looking out at the water. The lights bouncing off its surface looking positively magnificent, elegance radiating off the water in waves that leave me in silent awe. It makes me think of all the times I have been awake, this is by far the most beautiful time to be here. Technology is amazing, beautiful even, regardless of the fact that it is slowly destroying human's minds. A boat passes by as I stand there admiring the view and I watch as it floats on past, the people enjoying the ride not even noticing me. The wind blowing through my hair is simply refreshing as I marvel at the scene before me, the harsh contrast of gentle serenity brought from nature, struck so harshly with the physical abomination of manmade objects, the buildings reflected in the flowing water looking distorted as though nature its self is exacting its revenge for the unwelcome imprint on this view. Yet the different coloured lights seem to bounce around beautifully as though playing a game on the water's surface.

    I hear a sound behind me and instantly turn, sending out my senses to scan for danger. Finding nothing threatening I relax and return to watching the water, if it were someone to harm me they would have done so by now. I return my concentration to the tranquil view of lights dancing on the water and after a while I feel the warmth of a body next to me, but it feels so natural that it takes me a few moments to register it. I am only pulled out of my thoughts by the sound of his voice.

"It's a cold night Veronica, would you like my jacket?" Cole's calming voice surprises me, but I wince when he calls me Veronica, it feels so wrong to have him not know my real name. There is something about this man that has me so comfortable around him and yet so unusual.

"No, thank you Cole." my skin tingles again as I say his name and the look in his eyes has me wanting to kiss him again. I scold myself and turn to look back at the water, hoping for the same distraction I had moments ago. I can't help but feel frustrated when it doesn't work.

"So Veronica, I had a nice time at the club tonight." He says with his smooth confident voice saturating my body with a desire for his warmth.

"Really? Because I seem to recall you made a pretty quick exit." I say sarcastically and straight away think 'Violet what the hell are you doing? Are you seriously getting emotional over the fact that this man left you in a nightclub? That's what PEOPLE do, you are a vampire, so go be a frikking vampire!'

"You didn't want me to go?" his smile is arrogant and annoying, and I purse my lips at his audacity.

"That's not the point Cole, you can't say you had a nice time if you were the one that ended it. That's like shooting somebody and being surprised when they bleed." Now he turns to look back at the water, obviously avoiding my accusing stare.

"Well I suppose, allowing myself a moment of vulnerability here so I should get points for this, I had a little fright when I felt so connected with you. I have only ever felt like that once and it didn't end well. I admit I was scared off."

I gaze over the water trying to think of something to say, and all I can think about is who he felt connected to before and where is she now.

"It's a beautiful night, the river looks astonishing."

My thoughts shift to the kiss in the club and I start to feel fidgety, suddenly uncomfortable and anxious. What is it about this man that makes me feel all clumsy and foolish? And the tingles! What is with my skin tingling again? My breathing as well, yet again my breathing has sped up. I don't even need to breathe! I think it must be something to do with Veronica's life and emotions, her emotions were so strong they are still controlling the parts of the body I don't need. Whatever it is its rather annoying, I feel my toes curl in my boots as my fingers start fidgeting with the bottom of my top. I remember the way I almost fell because my knees buckled and Cole caught me, and that was how it started. The effect he has on me is almost frightening.

"Cole, I don't know what's going on here." I whisper deciding to come clean. "My body feels weird when you're around and I'm not used to it. I don't know how to make sense of everything I'm feeling." I turn to face him trying to find the words to explain that I need him to stay away from me. How can I explain to him that I need a clear head while I save the world without him thinking I'm crazy!

Before I can say anything else his hands are on my arms, his forehead pressed against mine with his eyes closed.

"Veronica I can't help you understand because I am finding myself in exactly the same predicament. Being around you even for the shortest time I feel free, more free than I have ever felt before."

He kisses me, his lips take over my thoughts and my hands go to his hair. I am pulled back into the paradise he took me to in the club and I don't care anymore, about anything. Nature has brought us together twice within the space of twenty four hours, it must want this.

He walks forwards pushing me backwards until my back collides with a tree. His hands move to my hips, thumbs caressing the skin of my abdomen between the bottom of my top and top of bottoms sending shivers down my spine. I open my lips as a whimper of pleasure escapes and his tongue thrusts inside my mouth, taking control. I gasp as his hand snakes around to my bottom and squeezes, pushing me closer to him. I feel his manhood against my stomach and cry out with need. My hips move against him and I stand on my toes to make the growing hardness digging into my stomach go lower and lower. I suddenly need closeness, I yearn for intimacy. All the frustration of lonely centuries built up exploding inside me all at once and I start pushing against him, putting my hands on his hips. I ride my hands up his sides bringing his shirt up and feel the soft warm flesh beneath. He giggles a little as I trace my fingers across his finely toned stomach lightly and I smile against his lips. I move my hands back to his sides and round to his back where my nails start to scratch him. His entire body shudders and he groans lightly, pulling me harder, closer and kissing me more passionately. I start to lift his top up his chest to take it off when the sound of someone clearing there throat loudly distracts us and brings us both crashing back to reality.

Pulling away from Cole disorientated and

confused I see Brian standing in front of us staring. Oh this isn't going to end well, Brian has always had a thing for me, no matter what body I take when I awake he has always made his feelings clear and I have always told him I have no interest in sex or relationships, or intimacy of any kind. So this should be fun then!

"Am I interrupting something?" Brian asks angrily

"Actually mate, yes you kind of are. Can we help you?" Cole says directly to him with an angry look on his face, not knowing that Brian is a vampire and will probably squish him like an insect if given the chance.

"I'm here to meet Violet, I didn't realise it was a first come first serve situation."

"I didn't say I would meet you Brian you went off on your own, and if you don't mind this has absolutely nothing to do with you so yes you are interrupting." He just stares at me and I think I see something almost threatening flash across his eyes.

"Oh I am sorry, I just thought we had more important stuff to do than having sex on a river bank. I hadn't realised you were so cheap and easy, maybe if I had stayed and gone with you you might have been able to keep yourself calm and focus on what we are doing."

"We were not having sex! And how dare you speak to me like this, it is none of your concern Brian so walk away."

"Oh no, I won't let you out of my site again Violet. Who knows who will jump you next." he turns and focuses on Cole, his eyes daring him to say something.

"Violet?" Cole asks eventually with a bitterness

AWAKE AGAIN

in his voice and I remember I told him my name was Veronica.

"Oh that is the cherry on top isn't it Violet, he didn't even remember your name. Well this is very interesting indeed." An evil grin lights Brian's face as he doesn't even bother to attempt to hide the sneering attitude.

"Cole I....." I try to think of something to say but I don't get the chance.

"Cole, I suggest you turn around and walk away now. Sorry but you aren't getting laid tonight pal so go try somewhere else."

"Brian!" I scold. But it is unheard.

"OK. Brian is it? I'm going to do you a real big favour. First of all I'm going to forget what you have said. Secondly I'm going to give you to the count of three to get out of my site before I get you the fuck out of it. I will warn you however, you have no idea what you are dealing with." His tone is hard but I know he doesn't stand a chance, a human against a vampire? The thought that Brian might hurt Cole has me gasping and about to step in.

Brian laughs as he walks in a circle around Cole, grabbing his fingers and pulling them behind his back in a move meant to immobilize and break the fingers as panic attaches itself to my heart for Cole. But it is quickly wiped away when I see Cole still standing. He hasn't moved at all, Brian hasn't even managed to get Cole's hand behind his back let alone break his fingers, Cole just stands there staring at me not even raising an eye brow as Brian desperately tries to immobilize him. After a moment Cole turns his head to look at Brian.

"Are you finished yet?" I see the horror on Brian's face, the excitement on Cole's, and my knees threaten to buckle again this time for a completely different reason. I feel like I could choke on thin air alone. In the blink of an eye Cole has done the exact move to Brian that seconds before was disturbingly difficult to watch. Now panic has me and it is not letting go. I hear a snap and Brian yelps, Cole just broke his arm! It will heal straight away, but the frightening part was that he could!

The only beings I cannot sense are the extremely powerful ones, and it hits me like a tonne of bricks. *Cole is a demon.* Tears sting my eyes but I push them away.

"Stop!" I yell and to all of our surprise he does. Brian looks at me awaiting an order, I am the leader after all and this situation requires leader ship.

"Brian I think you have to go, now!" I order and he actually does as he is told for once. Watching him walk quickly away I try to figure out what I am going to say to Cole, if he doesn't kill me that is!

"So, Violet the vampire." he spits, I look up to see his face. He is shocked and for a second I raise my hand about to stroke his cheek, but I pause realising what I was about to do and bite my lip. He looks hurt as I turn away from him with my eyes closed.

"Why couldn't I sense you?" his voice is low and I can barely hear him "I sensed *him* straight away, well after you had distracted me of course." he starts laughing bitterly and then stops, staring at me with conviction. "You distracted me on purpose! This whole thing is to find out what my plan is, you were going to worm your way in and probably stab me in the back!" he huffs. I stare at the water not really listening, when suddenly something clicks and it's my turn to be shocked.

"Your plan? Oh no, don't tell me that you're the threat?" I shake, my voice rising.

"You didn't know? How is this even possible? How could this even happen." he points from me to himself "Between us, you being a vampire and me being a demon. You here to save the world and me here to destroy it. Of all the souls and beings on this planet how could this happen?" his words sound harsh with his voice dripping viciousness. But I don't even care, he is the threat.

In all the times I have walked the earth I have never been interested in sex or love and now I find myself all flustered over the enemy!

"Violet, what does this mean?" he asks desperately, and I can't answer. My voice won't work, my head is shaking and my lips aren't moving. The only thing that works are my legs, and I hadn't even noticed they had been running. I am far away from the river bank and Cole by the time I collapse to the floor and cry to myself.

SUSAN HATTON

Chapter 6

I enter Ally's home again just as the sun begins to rise behind me, light cascading over the doorway almost as though I'm taking the darkness with me. The smell of pancakes reaches my nose and in the back of my mind I wonder how I knew what pancakes are or even what they smell like. Clara greets me with a warm smile from behind the kitchen counter cooking and looking rather busy. Plated up on the counter are pancakes, eggs and bacon, fresh orange juice, toast and a newspaper.

"Sometimes I think you might miss cooking." I smile at her and she grins.

"I'm saying thank you to Ally, in the only way I know how, for letting us use her home as a safe house." And sure enough Ally walks down the stairs at the exact moment Clara has taken the apron off.

"Wow. This looks amazing thanks." She exclaims sitting down at the counter and digging in. She already knows it's for her since none of us eat.

Clara looks happy watching Ally dig in to her breakfast and I see the instinct in her excel with pride. Clara was born to be a mother and everyone in the group knows it. She is the mother of the group really, berating us when we do something she doesn't approve of or worrying when one of us is late meeting the others at all. But vampires cannot have children, so she waits patiently to be reborn.

But her purpose in existence has brought her here, into the warrior way of life, so like the rest of us she must sit back and find a way to cope. She knows as well as we do that the greater the sacrifice you make the greater the rewards will be.

As I'm watching her I feel a breeze behind me causing me to turn around, and I find myself face to face with Brian looking extremely angry.

"Well? What did lover boy have to say last night?"

"Ohhh you ran into Cole again?" Ally asks with a grin and a knowing wink.

Brian's eyebrows raise up in question.

"Again?"

"You guys we need to talk." I say and turn my back on Brian focusing on the rest of the group, yet before I say another word Brian beats me to it.

"Violet was with a demon tonight. I found her with him. All over each other. Practically fucking in the grass." His words are accusing as though I was caught giving the enemy all their names and where to find them, and part of me doesn't blame him since to him that is probably exactly how it looked.

"BRIAN!"

"Well you were, do you deny kissing him? Or trying to take his top off in a public place?"

"No I don't deny it, but you are being tactless and crude and I ORDER you to stop. NOW!" As I raise my voice to emphasise my word she leaves the room shaking his head and mumbling to himself. Defeated, but his purpose fulfilled.

"So you wanna fill us in on the details?" asks Ally between mouthfuls of pancake.

"I met Cole in a club just after I awoke." I begin explaining after everyone has sat down. "And I can't explain it but it was like we were drawn to each other. It was overwhelming, I didn't understand what my body was doing. The urges took over and before I knew it we were kissing and I don't even know who made the first move! I didn't want to say anything before because I thought I was just being silly. Anyway, I kind of ran into him again and the whole thing started to happen again. We lost ourselves, it was like being with him made the world right. Then Brian turned up and got all jealous, and after a bit of a fight we found out Cole is a demon. And I don't know what it means, or what happens now." I throw my hands up in frustration met only with confused looks from the group when I hoped one person would stand and tell me exactly what was happening.

"We need more information than that." Clara said.

"I have no more information!"

"Then we can't help you figure this one out I'm afraid." Her hand reaches out and strokes my arm gently letting me know that although they can't help me, they wish they could. That in its self helps to raise my spirits, I have already learnt that a lot of people don't have the kind of friends I do.

"But you have never been interested in love, why now?" George asks from the back of the group, too caught up in his own curiosity to forget he is in a room full of people, quickly shrinking into himself once more. Clara puts her arm around him to warm him, he has always been rather shy when it came to his curiosity and asking questions.

"There is more. He mentioned something about a plan, he thought I was trying to distract him on purpose. Cole is the threat. "Now my words take on a harsh edge as I fight back the emotion I feel welling up inside, I can't be doing a good job of hiding it however since Clara bounced her way over and enveloped me in the tightest, warmest hug I have ever had!

"There is talk of 'angel hunting' going on." Says Brian from the doorway causing everyone in the room to gasp, Clara's hand remaining on my back giving me strength just when I need it most. "Oh yeah, I went to see one of MY friends last night. I was actually working and found some stuff out. You know like we were supposed to? Seems lover boy is planning on taking an angel as his prisoner and absorbing its power. I don't know how but if we are here then it must be possible." The colour drains from my face, his words stabbing at my heart. He wants to keep an angel against their will? I thought you could only absorb an angel's power if you killed them, and you can't kill an angel! Can you? Oh no ….

"Why were you so desperate to go off on your own? Who did you see?" I ask him feeling slightly uneasy, almost suspicious.

"Because I knew as soon as I walked in here yesterday that there was something different about you this time and I can't trust you anymore. Now I know that you are in league with the enemy! As for my friend, well you have your secrets and I have mine." He spits at me.

"I have most definatly NOT switched sides!"

"We need to find out more, and I think it's about time we discuss Violet handing over command." Brian stares at me and I, along with the rest of the group stare blankly back at him. "Well isn't it obvious? She is too involved. We can't trust her to make decisions with her head if she is involved with her groin!" Brian is trying to make the others doubt me and for a split second I think he might accomplish it, I wouldn't blame them for turning on me!

"Now hang on just a second, do any of you

really believe that I would put the rest of the world at risk over emotion?" I try not to let on that I am asking myself the very same question. After all I should have stayed when I realised it was him, I should have tried to kill him or at least pushed him for answers. But I just ran. At that moment in time the need to not know the truth outweighed the need to save the world.

Everyone, even Ally who isn't technically part of the group, nods at me and the words "Violet stays in charge." ring out around me. I sigh in relief as I know at least these guys haven't given up on me.

"So what do we do now Violet?" asks Clara and the others look expectantly at me.

"I guess we learn all we can about angels." Everyone looks from one person to the other, not really knowing where to start. Except Brian who yet again walks out of the room, shaking his head from side to side muttering under his breath. A trait quickly becoming all too familiar with him.

"I'll get the laptop." Ally says as though it should have been our first idea. And before we know it we are *googling* angels!

Ally types in the search bar 'How to kill an angel' and it brings up something called Wikipedia.

'Actually, while an angel is in mortal form on earth, they can be affected by one thing: Qeres. The Egyptians had a perfume called Qeres that was used during mummification to provide the first 'sweet breathe' of the afterlife. Qeres is an extremely rare substance because its recipe has been lost, but small amounts still exist. This perfume is a lethal poison to an angel (fallen or otherwise), and if poured over say, the blade of a knife, could in fact terminate an angel. While non lethal to humans, it can burn or

poison anyone who carries the nephilitic gene. (see Genesis 6). if you are still thinking that a nephilim died in the flood, think about Goliath, or King David's 'men of great re-known'. But yes, qeres can kill an angel. And no afterlife awaits them either.'

We all look at each other in shock, the thought that a mere perfume could kill an angel seems very difficult to believe indeed. An angel is powerful enough to keep themselves hidden from site. But who really knows?

"I'm just gonna write in 'Qeres' on the list of possible leads and put a question mark next to it." Clara nods at us and writes it down as Ally searches again.

A lot of results appear for television shows or books, or names of companies and it is hard work sifting through them all.

After another few hours on the laptop we look again to the list of possible leads.

- Qeres. ?
- Cause an angel to sin and go crazy.
- Wish I was human so I could have a sand which.
- A weapon made by Lucifer and dipped in the blood of unicorns.
- I wonder how much more stuff I can write down before they want to check this.
- Something about cut off their wings and they are mortal.
- Halos. This is a bad joke.
- Have an angel google how to kill angels and bore it to death.

We all look to Clara.

"What?" she asks innocently. "This is ridiculous, how on earth are we going to find out how to kill an angel if these people don't even know what an angel is anymore! They think an angel is some sort of winged messenger from god! I mean seriously this is hopeless. We should be out there searching and finding things not in here wasting our time." She throws her pen down and we can all see that this is a big deal to Clara and I think I know why.

Angels are the souls of children that died young. It was there purpose to depart their bodies for one reason or another and as a way of apology for that nature has granted them the power to remain in a state of play until they are re-incarnated hiding them from all humans and beings and protecting them from danger, sorrow or pain. The world in which their souls rest is like a giant playground and they will never know unhappiness. Their power keeps them on the swings in the park, or picking flowers in a beautiful meadow, or climbing to the very tallest bar on the climbing frame, or eating the biggest mountain of ice cream ever. What we call the protectors, souls in need of someone to care for, watch over them and help them to move on when it is time. Clara really wanted children. Of course it is impossible now for her to have children but I fear this entire operation has more meaning than protecting the world to her, I think now she just wants to protect the children. I leave her to it, she may not be trying to save the world any more but indirectly her cause is the same as ours.

"I think Clara's right we need to be out there, this internet thing isn't doing us much good there's only been one or two things that could *possibly* kill an angel so far!"

"Hang on." Says Ally quietly, and we all turn to her realising while we had all given up and were about to leave the table she had been mesmerised by the computer screen. "Listen to this." she says.

'As the angel before you plays her games and her sister laughs and squeals,

Chant the words you know so well and to them you shall appeal,

To them a man will be seen with a kind and gentle smile,

Be quick you will and take them there it only lasts awhile,

A prison you need a cage it will be, deep within their minds,

To believe you they must, you have to protect them for dangers are outside,

The weapon you need is within them you see it is their own demise,

A stone they will give but mortality you will take as you look into their eyes,

The place go now with the weapon you need, your task you have accomplished,

And rule the world with all the power you have now it is finished.'

My mouth is open in horror, staring at Ally as her eye's search the screen desperately.

"It's gone." she whispers, sitting back with confusion on her face. "The screen popped up with the words and now it's gone, pretty much as soon as I finished reading it." she is shaking her head in disbelief.

Nature has been known to help us along from

time to time but this is a lot more obvious than anything ever before. We know instantly we are running out of time. After a minutes hesitation we all begin walking and organising before sitting with more sheets of paper writing down the words before we forget anything. Then we start making sense of it as Ally begins getting ready for work.

"*As the angel before you plays her games and her sister laughs and squeals.* So he is looking for sisters. How is he finding them? Do we know of any way to see an angel? Or search for one or even smell one?" we have to start sifting through this one bit at a time, we need to be able to see angels as well if we are to rescue them.

"I once heard about luring angels but I don't know about seeing them." says George.

"Luring them?" I ask shocked again. It's hard to believe anybody would want to lure an angel to harm.

"Yes, a cloaking spell so you basically look like an ice cream man and tell them you have some surprises for them and they have to follow you. A bit more complex obviously but you get the point." he explains and I shiver coldly along with the others.

"OK so we think he is going to kidnap two angels, keep them as his prisoners so that he can kill them and absorb their power and rule the world. When are you seeing him again then Violet?" Brian shoots between his teeth making me cringe. I am thank full to Clara who gives him a *very* sharp elbow to the ribs. I smile a thank you and she returns it.

"We all know sometimes love happens to the wrong people for the right reasons, I am the perfect example of forbidden love working out in the end." Ally's voice comes from the hallway filling me with happiness and hope that my situation could turn out somewhat like hers did.

"Anyway, so we think we have solved that part of the riddle, what's next?" I ask pointedly at Clara motioning for her to read the next part.

"Chant the words you know so well and to them you shall appeal,
To them a man will be seen with a kind and gentle smile,
Be quick you will and take them there it only lasts awhile."

"That sounds like the cloaking spell George mentioned, but it doesn't last long so he is timed for it?" George nods. "Well I suppose we could maybe try to see that as an upside and hope time is on our side rather than his."

"It takes a lot of power to do it so not only will he be timed for it but he will be weak for a while afterwards." This is good news!

"A prison you need a cage it will be, deep within their minds,
To believe you they must, you have to protect them for dangers are outside" Clara reads the next part, and we all look grim.

"He is going to imprison the angel sisters somewhere by telling them it's too dangerous for them to leave." and I feel the tears threatening my eyes, how could I have ever felt attracted to him? I am repulsed with myself.

"The weapon you need is within them you see it

is their own demise,
A stone they will give but mortality you will take as you look into their eyes"

She looks down as she reads this part, her own tears falling. I see Brian roll his eyes at her and I think how much I want to hurt him at that moment. This whole thing clearly has hidden depth for Clara, and he must start showing respect. This jealousy over me and Cole has gone far enough.

"The stone of power." George says under his breath. "I always thought it was a rumour. They say that nature gifts the children's souls with a stone of power either on a necklace or a bracelet or the handle of a toy sword, something the child will fall in love with and keep it with them always. The stone is what protects the soul, from everything. It's what keeps them out of our world but still on earth."

"George how do you know so much?" I ask.

"I listen." he says shrugging his shoulder. "I have always had a thing for magical creatures and warlocks and far off places, I was turned into a vampire after all that had fallen but I love listening to the tales when I am awake, I listen to you guys talk about old times and people or beings you knew. I spoke for a while with Ally last night about her memories. It all fascinates me, every time I have been on earth I have found a passion for listening, especially to others. The souls, after you wake them and they want to reminisce." he is getting nervous now with us all staring at him, rambling on about how he enjoys listening.

"George I think we have just found your purpose." I whisper to him and his eyes shoot up to meet mine, I'm vaguely aware of Brian scowling at me in the corner. "Your love of listening has brought forward the information we need. Thank you. Just for being you." I smile at him and he beams. I know he struggles a lot feeling like the odd one out since he is the youngest of the group and doesn't really know many old souls, memories from Veronica show me how it feels to be different. But it is so much better to be yourself and a little different than do your best to fit in with everyone else.

"Now what?" asks Brian menacingly, jealous yet again. He doesn't know his purpose and hates it when someone else finds theirs.

"Now Brian, I am going to get away from you before I take it upon myself to shut you up for good, and stop giving everyone evil looks just because you're a moody fucker you are pissing everyone off. Get over yourself." I stand and walk away ignoring the laughs from Clara and Damien! And I walk out the door.

Chapter 7

It is chilly outside but I don't feel it. I only know from the frost on the leaves and grass. I walk in the direction my feet take me, allowing the fresh air to enter my nose merely as a novelty. I stick to the streets this time, aware that open spaces make me more of a target and there is a demon out there. Although it angers me to find a tiny part of me that wishes Cole *would* find me. My thoughts are jumbled. How can he be so evil and yet make me feel so good. When he kissed me it was like I was floating, he managed to make me feel alone with him in a room full of people, the way my body swayed in rhythm with his as we danced, or the way the unnecessary breath left my body as he pinned me against the tree, the way I felt his need for me and my answering yearn to have his hands explore me. The tingles start in my toes as I walk and I know I need to stop thinking about him but I can't, the way he looked at me with his eyes searched mine as though trying to dig into my very soul, the way his fingertips brushed my back and made me moan in pleasure even though it confused me at the time. My mind is going round and round and suddenly everything stops.

The way he is going to trick the angels that he is going to kidnap. Picture it, two innocent girls shaking with fear trapped by a monster that plans to murder them. Yes he is brilliant, I wonder if that will be the last thought in your mind when he kills you. But he did seem interested in you, he might kill everyone else first and let you watch. What a fantastic weekend together that would be!

I stop the train on which my thoughts are headed as I feel the tears about to break free. I need open space. I climb the building I was leaning against and stand on the roof lifting my head and opening my eyes wide. Trying to trick myself into believing I am as strong inside as I am out.

I run, to the end of the building. When I get there I jump to the next, and the one after that. Picking up speed and telling myself I am strong and free. Strong and free. Run. Strong and free. Jump. I am strong. Run. I am free. Jump. I am a warrior. Run. I do not feel love. Jump. Emotions are weak. Love is not for vampires. Run. I am free. I am my own. I love nobody.

The memories are still flooding my mind and I run faster, chanting to myself as I run and jump over the buildings. Memories of his arms around my waist, the way he caught me on the dance floor when I nearly fell. He thought I was mortal. The look in his eyes when he discovered the truth. The horror that we couldn't be together at all.

Oh my, I think I do love him. But I can't. I couldn't possibly love someone that wants to harm angels. I stumble jumping, and I fall between the buildings grazing my shoulder, catching and breaking my ankle as I fall to the ground. Both are healed by the time I land but when I look up I freeze with fear. I am standing right in front of him. *Nature sucks.*

"Oh frig!" I say.

He looks shocked, I think I must have caught him doing something as he looked very annoyed before he saw who it was. I am aware of a sound of running behind me.

"Well, well, well. Violet, spying on me were you?" he accuses rather than asks.

"Not at all Cole, I was running. I slipped. Here I am. Please go about your business and I will try to only get in your way when it is time to kill you." I whisper with fake pleasantness, trying to remind myself that I shouldn't be feeling happy to see him.

"Oh but I was having fun with someone, I was just about to feed off her energy when you so rudely interrupted and scared he off. She was full of darkness, it would have made a very satisfying meal. You have cost me my supper now." He puts his hand beside my head, leaning on the wall behind me. I feel a twinge of jealousy when he says he was here with a woman but I do my best to push it down deep inside of me.

A tingling sensation courses through my legs as I know what he wants, and I answer him with a moan as his lips go to my neck. I know I shouldn't, I know I can't, but I know I don't want him to move away. He doesn't touch me, I just feel him. Not his mouth, not his tongue, not his fingers, just his breath. His energy is tantalising as I feel the soft tenderness of it caress my flesh ever so slightly. But it ignites all kinds of ideas in my mind. I'm panting for breath as he moves his head around at such close proximity I can actually smell the cotton in his tight fitting black shirt. Which I want to rip open.

"Now what do you suppose we do about this?" he raises his head and looks into my eyes, there's a darkness there that sends a wave of anticipation all throughout my body. The word 'Bond' in big bold letters flashing in my head. I start to squirm in anticipation as I notice his body shuddering as he tries to control himself.

"I think you had better stay still, angel." he whispers.

As though he had flicked on a light switch everything comes flooding back to me. My eyes open wider at the word 'Angel' and I recoil in horror. I move to push him away and his arms find mine, he grabs my wrists in one hand and holds them above my head so my elbows are bent at an awkward angle. There's no point fighting my arms free, I know I won't win. I start kicking my feet out attempting to catch him and distract him even if only for a second. He slots his knee between mine so I can hardly move my legs. I am pinned against the wall. Fear grips me and I think of Veronica with James in the alley. I look straight into Cole's eyes and spit in his face.

"You're disgusting." I say harshly, a twinge of guilt passes through me as I see his reaction but it doesn't last long. This demon wants to capture the souls of children and terrorise them. Before eventually killing them for power. The thought pulls the tears back to my eyes and I watch the confusion play on his face. His hands tighten on my wrists making me cry out in pain still unable to move my arms or legs at all, I use my words against him as best I can.

"Taking over the world, how pathetic. I can't believe I even felt anything for you!" his eyes really are wide now and as my eyes catch his I stop fighting. Everything stops. It's happening again. Damn it! His eyes are lost, mouth hanging open. Staring straight at me. I am losing myself in my own body, the sway of the dance floor coming back.

He places his free hand on my hip and gently traces the tip of his thumb over the skin under the flimsy top. Reminding me of when he pinned me against the tree, my body remembers the rhythm. The dance floor, the river bank and now this? Nature isn't just pushing us together its forcing us!

I swallow nervously, and his eyes dart to my throat. His lips open even further and his breathing changes. He leans forward and nudges my chin with the top of his head so my head is tilted backwards. His lips find my throat. Everything is turned upside down, I aren't even thinking about what he is or what he isn't. All I can focus on is what he is doing. My legs start to move but I'm not fighting any more. His tongue is skimming the flesh from the centre of my throat to the bottom of my ear and it feels good. Really good. Everywhere.

He moves his leg, the one between both of mine, rubbing harshly against my sensitive skin. I moan loudly. Before I know it his lips are on mine, tongue thrusting deep inside my mouth. My hands are free and in his hair pulling him to me as I feel his hands tighten on my hips, gripping me fiercely in a way that makes me shudder with excitement. My fingers run through his hair, nails digging into the flesh of his scalp needing to strengthen this connection, making him moan in return. My entire body is out of control, doing things I've never done and feeling things I've never felt.

I don't even realise I'm doing it but suddenly I have HIM pinned against the wall ripping his shirt from his body. I pull away from the kiss for a moment to appreciate his toned abdomen, the muscles, the skin tone, the warmth, the scars, I lean down and kiss his chest making him suck air between his teeth, growling low in his throat. I use my nail and gently make a little cut on his shoulder, watching mesmerised as a single drop of blood spills out.

This will bind us, so I always know where he is. I will always sense him after this, always know him, and always be with him.

The thought flitters though my mind as though it has been planted by nature, at this point I don't particularly care where it came from. I look up into his eyes again and I see him pleading with me, he really wants this as well. His breath is shaky, his eyes begging, and his hands still holding my hips. I lean down and use my tongue to clean the drop of blood from his flesh, he moans and I place my lips around the cut taking a small amount of him into myself.

When I pull away he is moaning loudly, he pulls me to him, our lips crashing together. He makes a cut on my breast moving his head down my neck, I didn't even notice him move my top or bra out of the way yet both breasts are exposed! His mouth goes around my cut as he returns the favour and it feels amazing. Everything goes weak, my limbs aren't my own any more. His hand cups my breast pushing it further into his mouth and a strange squeaking noise escapes my throat. My body feels like it's on fire, in a good way. The blood bond is working strong already and I feel an instant injection of pleasure. His fingers working circles on my nipples feels electrifying and the sensation moves to my legs, the muscles tensing and relaxing as a feeling of strengthened weakness washes all over me. How is it possible to feel absolutely everything and yet still nothing all at the same time? All I can see is the back of his head and still he looks magnificent, but as he finishes with my blood he replaces his fingers for his mouth around my nipple and an explosion happens within my body as he takes the nipple between his teeth, gently pulling and squeezing. I thrust my hips against his and he raises his head to kiss me again, his hands move to my behind, squeezing it and carrying on further to the backs of my thighs as he lifts me up. My legs automatically wrapping around his waist, my hands grabbing his face and pulling him closer, he slams me against the wall as he growls in his throat again.

I feel his erection rubbing against me and I pull his tongue into my mouth with my mine as he moves his hips against mine. I unwrap my legs from around him and stand, using the wall for support. I start to unbutton my trousers but he stops me, pulling my top over my breasts and picking up his shirt he leads me out of the alley way into a building.

The double glass doors close behind us revealing a large hotel lounge, with beautifully embroidered curtains dropping elegantly to the floor and forming small pools of material, patchwork chairs of all different colours, and a bar serving alcohol in the middle. This place is nothing like the club we were in before, there is no music blasting and no girls hardly wearing clothes. Some stairs on the right hand side lead down to a dining area and doors at the back I'm assuming lead to the rooms.

"Welcome, can I help you?" asks the woman behind the desk next to the entrance.

"We need a room."

"I'm afraid check in is over for today, I can book you in for tomorrow at the earliest." She answers Cole with her perfectly rehearsed tone.

"Not acceptable we need a room now. I will pay double."

"I'm afraid it doesn't work like that sir."

Cole leans over the desk and looks into her eyes, at first I think he must be performing some weird magic to control her mind but when he opens his mouth to speak his words are filled with more evil than I have ever known.

"If we don't get a room right now, I will purposely gut you and everyone in here. I will hang you by the neck at the door as a warning to all who enter."

"I'm so sorry, he needs his medicines and I'm afraid we are need of a bed to strap him down. The doctor said to expect a relapse if he doesn't take his pills on time." I say hurriedly.

"Of course, I do have a room available for an emergency but it has just been vacated. I expect a little mess is no problem right now." She starts typing away on her computer and hands over a key card. "Room 216, and don't worry about paying until you leave." Her hands are shaking as much as her voice is, and as soon as I take the key card she practically runs out of the room and slams the door. I expect she is probably crying in shock and fear and I can't help but give Cole a quick swipe in the back of the knee with my foot as I follow behind him to our room.

Chapter 8

"Violet what the hell is going on. This, you! You aren't part of the plan. I can't stop thinking about you." His words are loud and angry to start with but become nothing more than a soft whisper, as he closes the door behind me and walks towards me I get the strange sensation as though I'm weightless. "I can't concentrate when you're gone and when you're around all I can see is you!" I shake my head in wordless answer and wait for him to touch me again, but he stops just in front of me.

"I don't know Cole. I don't know what I'm doing, I don't know why I'm staying, I don't know why I bonded with you, I don't know why I went into that club, I don't know why I was mesmerised by the water, I don't know what my body is doing, I don't know why when I'm with you I struggle to breathe when I don't even need to breathe, I don't know why you make me feel human. All I know is that I get told to follow my instincts all the time, and that's what I am doing. My instincts have never been wrong before nor have they ever been this strong. And right now my instincts want you to throw me on that bed and show me exactly what I have been missing all these lonely centuries."

"Oh Jesus Christ!" he almost yells as again his body crashes against mine, his hands on the buttons of my jeans and his lips on mine as he pulls me over to the bed. He turns me around so the bed is behind me, lifting my top over my head and throwing it to the floor. He drops my jeans and pushes back on to the bed, he removes his own clothes and discards them very quickly.

When he looks back at me he freezes. His mouth stuck open as he stares at me. I can't imagine the view being all that great I mean yes the white lacy underwear I found in Veronicas drawer are pretty but surely the big black socks are a put off! I quickly remove them and my bra and he laughs at me. For some reason I want him to take off the thin scrap of material left covering the last bit of flesh on my body. The part of my flesh that is currently hot and throbbing with need for him.

He grabs my ankle in one hand and raises it to his shoulder, where he plants soft kisses. Then he kneels on the end of the bed and moves his mouth further and further up my leg to the inside of my thigh. My eyes are closed in nervous expectation as my mouth is opening and closing, my tongue darting out to moisten my suddenly dry lips.

He stops when he reaches the top ignoring my moans of protest, takes my other ankle and starts the agonisingly slow process again on my other leg. By now I'm squirming on the bed with my fingers splayed and grabbing fistfuls of quilt, lifting my hips off the bed eagerly begging for closeness. When his lips go all the way up the inside of my thigh I whisper his name, urging him to continue. He snakes his hands around my thighs and slowly and wickedly kisses me over the lace. His hot breath heating up the material on my vulva and delighting my senses even more. All different sensations and emotions are being felt through one intimate act.

My soul is a virgin but Veronica was a prostitute, so I know a bit about sex from her memories, and at least my first time won't hurt. He pulls down my underwear until they are at my knees and leaves them there, kissing the tops of my thighs while his hands massage my knees. He puts his head between my legs and I feel his tongue on my clitoris, my hips are going up and down begging for him to enter me and he keeps going with his delicious tongue until my body writhes beneath him, he removes my underwear completely and opens my legs, one of his hands moves away from my knee and I feel him playing, inserting a finger in and out, in and out and round, making me moist. Now I'm almost screaming for him to take me. Rolling around on the bed probably looking as sexy as a fish out of water but I don't care, I can't care!

"Please, Cole please, I don't care about anything else right now I just need you. Just you please Cole. Love me." With a moan as though he can't take it any longer he moves on top of me, eyes on mine as he puts the tip of his manhood to my opening.

"Are you sure?" he whispers and straight away he looks surprised that even asked it! I gasp as I encase him in my arms and bring him down closer to me, thrusting my hips up to meet him as he enters me. I groan in pleasure as I kiss his neck, biting him and nibbling his skin.

"Yes this is it, this all we need. We only need each other. Like this. Nothing else. Nothing else matters." I can feel the tears on my cheeks but I can't stop them, like this I love him. Right in this moment he is my everything and nobody can destroy this, I want to protect him, and be protected *by* him. He is my purpose I just know it.

"Violet, oh Violet!" he whispers with so much emotion I can't help but embrace him tighter, responding to my breathless ranting by thrusting deeper. I feel it too, the need to be even closer, as close as we can get. He sits up on his knees and pulls me up, holding me in his arms and kissing my neck and chest as he thrusts in and out. His hands move to my hips moving me up and down and I feel my muscles tense and relax, my arms around his neck tightening as I build to climax. Hands going wild in his hair as my body takes over a completely new rhythm of love and ecstasy and my legs begin to move, my hips moving perfectly in time with his.

Our thrusts become more urgent, faster and harder, as his breathing is shaking. His fingertips dig into the flesh on my hips, the blood bond working so we feel each other's pleasure as well as our own.

"Holy shit Violet, what are you doing to me?" he asks under his breath though I know he doesn't really want an answer.

"Oh Cole, Oh yes." I scream as I feel my climax explode around him. He carries on thrusting, the whole time I'm screaming his name he is still going fast and hard and while already in the throes of orgasm I sense another one on its way as well.

"Again, scream my name again. For the love of god say my name." he is kissing my chest moving from one breast to the next.

"Cole!" I scream once, and he is deep inside me. Thrusting deeper, deeper, his mouth on my skin, biting me and holding me down while aggressively thrusting and yelling my name through his teeth.

He collapses on the bed when he is finished, his hands are around my waist shaking with the force of his orgasm. He is still inside me as deep as possible and I feel him pulse and emptying. My muscles electrocuted and on edge. We lay there for ages, me in his arms. Not wanting to talk, to ruin it at all. I shut my eyes and remember what dreaming used to be like.

"Violet?" I hear the voice from the doorway and we both shoot up, still naked on the bed. Brian is standing in the door way with pure horror on his face. "You gonna try telling me you're not fucking the enemy?"
"Oh hell." I say, knowing the damage this will do.
"What the fuck are you doing in here?" asks Cole, I can tell instantly from his tone that he is pissed.
"Cole it's OK I can handle this." I soothe him with a hand on his arm.
"So what the fuck is this exactly?" Brian asks harshly as Cole passes me a sheet to cover my body with, before standing and walking away to find his clothes. Brian walks into the room without invitation and sits himself down in an arm chair facing us, bringing his right foot to rest on his left knee cap and holding his hands together under his chin, waiting eagerly for an explanation.
"Brian this has nothing to do with you, you are out of order. Leave." I let a little touch of menace into my voice to let him know just how serious I am, but he doesn't listen, instead he just stares at me with a weird smile on his face.
"So then Violet, finally did it then. Oh did you know it was her first time?" he asks Cole who just stares at me with his mouth hanging open. "Yeah that's right she gave you her flower. Sweet ain't it." He says mocking me.
"I think you had better remember your place Brian." Cole has his back to Brian, still only wearing

his jeans showing the perfect muscles of his back, and I struggle to stay in control of my senses for a moment.

"Well it's easy to remember your place isn't it Demon. Under her. Or over her. Whichever." he sniggers like an errant teenager and Cole actually hisses from the other side of the room, moving his head from one side of his neck to the other in a stretching rolling motion that makes me think things are about to get out of control!

"Brian get out before I throw you out. This has nothing to do with you so take your jealousy and hurt pride and walk the fuck away. I think it is time you left the group." He stands up and looks blankly at me.

"Knew it was only a matter of time before you switched sides. He has you brainwashed he does, you belong with me Violet and you know it so why do you keep fighting it?" I don't even get to answer before Cole tackles him, throwing him down to the ground with such a bang I would be surprised if the ceiling is still intact in the room below us!

I jump off the bed and try to separate them, but in the process Brian accidentally hits me instead of Cole and breaks my nose. It only bleeds for a second before fixing itself and I barely even notice the pain. Brian and Cole how ever stop immediately; as men do when a woman is hurt. Cole rushes to my side and checks I am OK. Brian cowers away, falling backwards over the chair and still moving away from him. He hadn't forgotten who I am, but he knew I wouldn't do anything to let my full potential out just because someone was getting sassy with his words. He can see in my eyes right now though that things have changed. With one simple move I have him pinned by the throat, finger nails drawing blood from his flesh as the sheet drops and reveals my naked body. Cole gasps from behind me as the red fire licks up my body from my legs to the hand pinning Brian. Brian howls in pain.

"You were given warnings, you were given chances. Here is your final choice." My voice is amplified in the small room and I am so fixated on Brian I don't even notice Cole walking over to investigate. "You leave, walk away, now. And never return. Or…" I let the fire circulating my arm caress his cheek and drop him to the ground crying out in pain and shaking with fear. He quickly manoeuvres around me and clearly understands the danger he is facing, actually bowing as he runs out of the room away from me.

"Who the fuck are you Violet?" Cole asks laughing as though he just found out I am part of the royal family or something, fingers tracing my skin where the fire disappears. He wraps the sheet back around my body carefully and leads me over to sit on the bed with him.

It takes me a few minutes to decide whether or not I should tell him the truth, but in the end I know I can't lie to him again. "I am the first vampire." I say simply and his face falls. All of the magical beings know of me, I am the most powerful of all vampires. Not magically but physically. The group know who I am, as does Alliyana but it is not something I advertise.

"Wow. And what is this group?" he asks casually while lifting the chair up off the floor and trying to put the room back in order.

"My friends, we are blood bonded so we can always find each other. We are the only ones to work together for every awakening. We find each other then we find the threat. I can't explain why, because I don't really know why. We all just feel better being together. We assume our purposes are linked." As I say the last sentence we both stop and just look at each other, I am the first to break eye contact as I sit back on the bed.

"What do we do now?" He asks walking over and sitting next to me again, his hand going to my back and rubbing gently.

"Well we could always stay in here for ever, you're the threat and your still here so ultimately so am I." he laughs and holds me to him, I can't remember the last time I felt this safe.

"We could stay here one night." I suggest seriously and he pulls away, taking my chin in his hand and tilting my head to look at him. His jaw stern and eyes shadowed as though something is tearing him up inside much the same way something is tearing me up inside.

"Is that what you would like?" I nod my head yes and his face relaxes. "And this was really you're first time?" A second nod has him closing his eyes and shaking his head, whispering the word sorry as he kisses my forehead.

"I have been an animal. I drag you in here, have my way with you, and didn't even consider you hadn't… you know!"

"What's the matter?" I am so confused by his words I can't stop myself from frowning at him. "I thought it was perfect!"

He picks up a remote control from the stand by the bed and flicks the television on, then he lifts the phone and sits right back on the bed against the headboard still wearing only his jeans.

"I won't be long you go enjoy a shower or a

bath. I bet those are luxuries you haven't experienced in a long time." he starts talking to someone on the phone and I give up trying to find out what he meant and walk into the bathroom exploring the white and black tiled room.

I see something sticking out of the ceiling with some buttons and funny shaped bits of metal on the wall below it, and when I turn them water falls from the ceiling like a water fall. I squeal and laugh as I become drenched from head to foot. Cole stands in the doorway watching me and when he laughs I walk out from under the water.

"What's so funny?" I ask him and he puts his head down in his hand.

"You're supposed to be naked." he points to the material still wrapped around my body, now wet and clinging to my skin.

"Oh." I say and drop it to the floor before stepping back under the water.

He stands there watching me, I can feel his eyes on my body. And it feels really weird, sort of sexy but at the same time I feel slightly self-conscious. After a minute he walks into the bathroom and lifts some small bottles next to the sink. He places them on the floor as he removes his jeans and joins me in the waterfall. Err... I mean the shower.

He picks up one of the bottles and squeezes some gooey stuff onto his hand, then he motions for me to turn around while he starts lathering the soapy liquid onto my body, I close my eyes and let him wash me feeling safe and relaxed.

"Food will be here in about 30 minutes." he says and I turn around to him confused.

"I didn't know you ate." I say.

"I don't, but tonight we both will."

"Cole, I can't!" I say. He doesn't understand not only do I not need to eat I physically do not want to. Oh I want to want to eat, don't get me wrong I am desperate to try a big juicy burger. But as a warrior I can't eat. It just won't happen. If anything the body would probably throw it all back up again. Especially with all the ridiculous chemicals that are in food nowadays bulking it up to sell for more profit!

"Tonight darling we both will." And he holds me. We stand under the water together like that for ages and I close my eyes to the warmth. After a few minutes something feels odd, the water feels hotter on my suddenly delicate skin and I take a moment to adjust my senses, it's harder to get my breath under the water and it makes me realise that I *need* to catch my breath.

I start to think it is just the whole me being next to Cole thing again but it isn't, I actually struggle for breath. I find myself gasping for it and sticking my head out of the shower the same time as Cole does.

I look at him confused as he hands me a towel to dry my shivering body with. *Why the fuck are we shivering?* I think as I see Cole wrap a towel around his waist and shake his torso from the cold.

"I have gifted you with mortality for the night. Until we wake up tomorrow we are just humans enjoying ourselves." he answers the questioning look I give him with a shy smile, telling me without words that he really hopes I like the gift. And after a moment I throw my arms up, dropping the towel again, and jump on him. Only he isn't as strong anymore, or as balanced, and we both crash to the ground rather painfully. He groans in pain and I yelp as I catch my arm painfully on the ground.

"I don't think you will make a very safe

human." He accuses and we both lay on the bathroom floor together laughing.

Chapter 9

We hear a knock on the door and both shoot up, I look at Cole worriedly thinking we are vulnerable now that we are mortal but he smiles reassuringly and hands me my towel.

"Foods here." He walks out of the bathroom to let them in. Jeez how long were we laid on the floor!

I walk out of the bathroom with the towel wrapped around me and see a man wheeling a trolley out of the room. He smiles shyly as he walks straight past me, my cheeks burn from the blush that spreads across my face. Cole smiles at me and I see he has put his jeans back on. He sits down at a table covered with plates, metal dome things on top to keep the food warm. I sit opposite him and lift my legs on to his knees under the table. This isn't a sex thing it is an intimacy thing, and it feels so right.

He uncovers all of the plates each one looking more spectacular than the last, we take a folk each and start tasting the modern day food not caring about anything at all. For one entire night we will simply be.

He eventually settles on eating with one hand, his other hand reaching under the table and warmly rubbing my feet. I smile at him with a mouthful of garlic bread and he laughs at me.

"You have herbs on your teeth." he says simply and I widen my eyes while covering my mouth, aware this is supposed to be embarrassing but I can't stop laughing.

"Champagne?" Cole asks me handing me a glass.

"Why Cole, are you trying to get me drunk?"

"What is it with vampires always accusing me of getting them drunk?" He says sarcastically and I laugh really hard now, a snorting noise coming from my nose as I struggle to laugh and breathe at the same time.

"Can you imagine a drunk vampire?" I ask him through giggle fits.

"As much as I can imagine a drunk Demon."

"A drunk, clumsy, snorting vampire!" He throws his head back in laughter. Pushing one foot against a leg of the table until he topples over the back of the chair completely. I can't help but join him with the gut wrenching hysterics when suddenly I'm struck by a strange and unfamiliar urge. The desperation very obvious and I start to giggle again, standing up and almost running into the bathroom and locking the door behind me.

"You OK?" he asks still laughing.

"Yes I am fine you just nearly made me pee myself!" I tell him the truth, feeling unbelievably human and I can't believe it will last for an entire night! "I will be out in a minute." I say and turn back to look at the toilet, I try to scan Veronicas memories for how to use it but find now I am human I am left on my own to figure it out!

When I'm done with the toilet I spend a few moments trying to work out the tap so I can wash my hands, but in the end I give in and turn the shower back on, washing them quickly underneath the water fall.

I walk back into the room to find Cole gasping and fanning his mouth, I am on instant alert for danger remembering we are mortal, and the panic strikes even more.

"Cole? What's wrong? What happened?" my voice raising as I begin to worry we are in danger, I run over to him while looking all around us for anything I can use as a weapon.

"Spicy pizza!" he answers gulping a full glass of water and laughing at me, his eyes red with tears threatening. I relax and sit back down.

"Strawberry Cheesecake. Eat that and drink champagne. Apparently it's amazing together." he says and picks up his pizza again making me laugh as yet again he starts fanning his mouth with his hand and fidgeting.

"Pizza nice then?" I ask calmly.

"Mm-hmm." he answers unable to actually speak.

I take a bite of cheese cake and moan almost the same way I do when Cole touches me. I close my eyes and focus solely on the taste for a while. When I open them Cole is staring at me, darkness in his eyes that has my stomach tightening.

"God that looks good, take another bite." I get the feeling his shaking voice is not caused by the pizza this time! I do it again this time pouting my lips and staring at him, trying to be as seductive as I can.

"What would you like to do now?" he asks me leaving his chair and kneeling on the floor in front of me.

"What are my options?" I ask huskily, again attempting sexiness as I watch him through my eye lashes. I lift the folk to my lips once more but before I put the cheesecake in my mouth his hand grabs my wrist stopping me. He leans forward and puts it in his own mouth, then turns to me looking innocent. Making me smile but slant my eyes at him.

"Thief!" I accuse. He places his hand on his

heart and opens his eyes wide, swallowing before opening his mouth to speak.

"Me? Never. I would never do such a thing!" he puts his hand under my arm and hoists me up over his shoulder. I kick and scream and laugh until he eventually puts me back down on my feet, folk still in hand. He takes it away laughing again and throws it on the table.

"What do you want to do?" he puts the seductive tone in his voice now and his hands find mine, putting them both behind my back so my breasts stick out against his chest, my nipples hardening and rubbing against the towel wrapping my body. He grasps both wrists in one hand, and with his other starts massaging my bottom, letting me know exactly what he wants to do. I get a weird feeling, and before I can answer him I am overtaken with it. I can't breathe, my nose feels suffocated as though someone is holding a pillow to my face. I inhale sharply a few times but it feels forced. I start to panic as thoughts of danger cloud my mind, I don't know what's happening.

Before I can do anything or work anything there's an explosion of snot and spit inside my head and I have just enough time to put my head down to stop projection heading straight for Cole's face.

He starts laughing at me and walks away bringing me some tissues.

"It's a bit disgusting being human again isn't it?" he asks still laughing.

"But still wonderful." My words sound funny as I try to talk past the furry feeling in my nose.

"I haven't ever done this before. Always had the power but I always thought 'why would I ever want to turn back human?' now I know. Tonight is magical, more so without the magic. Snot and all!" he says and when I look up still with squinting eyes I see the childish excitement dancing in his. I join him in laughing as I blow my nose. Being a human sure is embarrassing!

"Can I have a dance?"

"Of course you can have a dance, you can have anything you want tonight." he says smoothly.

"I just want a dance." I wait for him to put the music channels on the small television as I go back to eating cheesecake and drinking champagne at the table.

He walks over to me and offers me his hand, I take it smiling and as I stand he wraps the sheet from earlier around my body, tucking it over my shoulder and into the back, making it look almost like a beautiful ball gown.

"Wow I look almost elegant." I smile, and then laugh yet again.

"Ah my tactic of getting you drunk worked I see, I guess it's almost time to torture you for information." he says with a slightly sexy smile and my knees go weak.

"Oh I don't know if you're capable of torture. In fact for a Demon you're awfully sweet. It's probably more correct to say you would gently ease information from me by having cute little puppies lick my face." I tease him changing the way I speak to a more innocent tone, and he spins me again before dipping me down, yet again I find myself wondering how he manages to make the respectful dance suit the upbeat music.

"Is that right?" he asks me amused as he swiftly brings me back up to look at him, his leg in between mine so I feel every movement we make rubbing against the inside of my thighs. The dance becomes slightly less easy and a little more fast and hard.

"Yes that's right. I think you are completely besotted my darling Demon, love has captured your heart and I fear you may have fallen hard. The mere thought of me coming to harm causing your own breath to quicken and pulse to race. You despair in the thought of someone harming me, you wish to protect me until the very end. You wish to love me and cherish me and lavish me with affection." he smiles and dips me again, this time I feel his hand on my stomach holding me down as his breath tingles on my neck.

"That theory sounds mighty impressive my sweet, although I must say extremely detailed. Could we possibly be projecting our own feelings onto another?" I gasp as he hits the nail right on the head, I realise that what I said is in fact how I feel about him. He brings me back up and his eyes are on my mouth.

"Are we getting close to the truth?" he asks innocently as he spins me around and I moan at the sensation it brings as his leg thrusts forwards and backwards rubbing me gently and hard all at the same time.

"I'm not really sure, suddenly I am finding it a little difficult to concentrate." I say honestly and watch the victorious smile spread across his gloating face before he stands away from me clearly revelling in winning our playful word banter. "Oh I didn't mean to distract you." he says sheepishly. Well... two can play at that game!

"No, its fine. I seem to have recovered from my momentary lapse. Please continue." I ask him and this time I place my hands on his shoulders and let him place his hands on my hips, watching my body. "So where were we, oh that's right I was guessing how you feel about me which you have informed me I was wrong. So please Cole, tell me what is correct." as I look at him through my eye lashes again I press my breasts against his chest, and now *he* seems distracted.

"Well I don't know what to tell you Violet, you're just another notch on my bedpost." he smiles and leans in to kiss me but I move my head away.

"Oh Cole if only that were true, it would make things a whole lot easier for us wouldn't it." I point out to him and again he smiles and tries leaning in for a kiss. But again I move my head away.

"Violet, I am getting impatient." It sounds like a warning.

"Really? Why?" I act like I don't know what he is talking about and it seems to affect him in a rather sexual way. I simply shrug while I look at the longing in his eyes and I spin around, putting my back to him. "Cole how can I help you if I don't know what the problem is?" I ask still on a teasing rampage as I shake my hips slightly against his so my bottom rubs against him.

My move backfires though, I hear his breath through gritted teeth and the words "Oh fuck it." carry to my ears as he turns me around. In a very sexy aggressive way, his need for me turns me on. One hand cups my chin as he kisses me and the other hand is loosening the sheet. My own hands reaching forward for his jeans, desperation taking over completely as we both feel the need to merge our bodies as one.

We stand naked kissing for a moment, when he stops kissing me he brings his forehead to lean softly against mine and closes his eyes again.

AWAKE AGAIN

"Violet I think I love you." he whispers.

"Cole, I think I love you too." I answer and the tears fall down my face, when I open my eyes I see tears on his face, making me cry harder. We snot cry together as we both know exactly what it means when we wake up tomorrow.

He kisses me hard, and our tears and snot, all of our emotions merge together. And even with the disgusting grossness of it I am thrilled we both said it while humans. Nature wanted this and nature got it.

He carries me over to the bed and lays me down, quickly joining me under the covers so we can lay together as man and woman again both knowing all too well it won't last for much longer.

I try to force myself not to sleep, the spell will wear off when we wake up so if we don't go to sleep it never has to end. I haven't slept in thousands of years and the thought of it, of dreaming again, is heavenly. But it is shadowed with the horrid thought that me and Cole won't be together. We will be at war. I have to go back to destroying this evil, horrible, magnificent man who right now lays with his fingers interlocking with mine and kissing my back lovingly. Or he will destroy the world and kill everyone I care about. Including me. Or.......

The last thought I have before sleep consumes me is *'maybe this will persuade him to change his plans, maybe he won't want to be evil any more, maybe he could be as balanced as I am.'*

Chapter 10

When I wake up it isn't what I had imagined, I don't wake up with puffy eyes or stretching my muscles. I don't even blink at the brightness. My eyes are open and I'm awake. I'm a vampire again. No grogginess, no fuzzy head, no desperation for the bathroom. Nothing mortal what so ever. It's depressing. I look around for Cole but he has already gone. *Fuck. Here we go.*

I get dressed and leave the hotel room, knowing I have some explaining to do. I take a slow walk back to Ally's house and try to consider what I am going to say, and as I reach the door I decide honesty is the best policy. I open the door, and everyone is waiting around the breakfast table. They must have sensed me coming. Everyone looks extremely pissed off and I worry what lecture I'm going to receive.

"Oh Violet thank god your OK." Says Clara as she runs towards me and hugs me, surprising me.

Alliyana sits at the table looking tired. Has she been up all night?

"Yes we are so glad you are safe. Mind telling us what happened? We felt the bond break and thought you had been killed. Then we felt it return a short while ago." Damien walks around to stroke my arm warmly before taking Clara's hand and pulling her away from me. Clearly she is caught up in her emotions, her cheeks wet with tears.

"I'm sorry for worrying everyone. I bumped into Cole again, and we spent the night in a hotel together. I know it's crazy and I can't say why, but I think nature is pushing us together. We bonded, and then turned human for the night."

"That scoundrel! What did he do to you?" Ally shrieks.

"No it's not like that, he turned us *both* human. We had the entire night to just be a normal couple. He didn't hurt me."

"What like, human? Like mortal? What was it like?" asks Clara.

"It was embarrassing." I answer quickly recalling the rush for the toilet, trying to work out the taps, almost sneezing all over him and generally being clumsy. "But the cheesecake was good!"

"You ate food?" She yells at me in disbelief.

"Yes I did."

"I need more details!"

"We had a magical evening, one that prepared us to battle each other." And it's as though my words remind everyone of what we are doing. The excited eyes seem to dissipate as realisation sinks in. I am in love with a man whom I must kill, or he will kill me.

"Brian stopped by." Says George. "Said he was leaving and that we were fools if we didn't go with him. Wouldn't stop going on about how you stabbed us all in the back. We don't think you stabbed us in the back Violet, we think you might be finding your purpose. Remember you always have our support. Don't ever feel like you have to keep secrets from us." he says kindly, reassuring me and bringing me so close to tears I have to bite my lip.

"Thank you, Brian is angry with me because I told him to leave the group. He walked into the hotel room last night to see me and Cole together, and he made his opinion more than clear."

"So did you find anything out then?" Asks

Damien.

"No I did not." I reply grinning remembering how nothing at all was business.

"So you had a night not being a warrior at all then. I bet it was magnificent." he says truly happy for me.

"It was." I whisper and he smiles encouragingly at me.

"Well sorry to burst the bubble but it's time to get back to business remember. Angel's souls at risk and all that jazz." Ally pipes up, she doesn't sound annoyed just worried.

"Of course." I answer sheepishly.

"The problem is we know he wants sisters but we have no idea how to get from here to the world of the angels. We know how he is going to take them but not how he is going to get to their world. You bonded with him?" George asks me curiously and I nod. "Then I think you should try seeing just what you can do with that bond. We will work on getting us to the other realm and you work on the bond. No vampire has ever bonded with a Demon it could be very useful to us right now." He says it as a suggestion and I thank him with my smile, which he returns. He had seen I had no idea what to do and took over without actually taking over. He has such a sweet soul.

"OK you guys get googling or awakening old souls or something and I will go to some place quiet and see what I can do with this bond." I say walking out of the room as everyone turns back to Ally for the laptop.

I walk out of the house and again search for water. I make my way back to the same spot on the river bank me and Cole were at before, thinking it may be easier to home in on him if I am somewhere that reminds me of him. Its light out, there are people walking their dogs and playing with their children. I see a bench and sit down watching the tranquil view.

I close my eyes and send out my senses for Cole, but I get nothing back. I search for hours but still nothing, people go past and watch me curiously but it doesn't bother me.

Suddenly I'm opening my eyes to see the inside of a building, which wasn't there when I closed them! This must be what he is seeing. There are a number of children aligning one wall down a rather old fashioned corridor, and I can see they are all handcuffed to the radiators! My first thought is that these are angels, my heart is in my throat thinking that he could have kidnapped so many angels without us feeling a single change. A choking noise escapes me and I throw myself at the first child, trying to remove the chain but nothing happens, I can't feel it. None of the children even look at me. They all look malnourished, seriously. Wearing old clothes if any at all.

Some are curled up on the floor in front of the radiator. Three or four children to each pipe. Huddled together for warmth as the radiators aren't turned on yet there is frost on the inside of the windows. A group of children seem to be playing a game. And as I get closer my heart melts, listening to their game of 'count the floor boards'. These boy's must only be about 8 or 9 years old, and I notice then they seem to be grouped by age. A group of smaller children around a radiator further down and bigger children around the one I walked past. They count the floor boards, while the younger children count how many holes are in the walls.

I hear footsteps from a door at the end of the

corridor and a man appears followed by a small dumpy woman with keys. When the children hear the noise of the door opening they flinch.

"Cole, Lee and Ryan." he says and she walks over to the other older boys behind me, my breath catches as I hear the names and I stare at the boys. One of them is taller, with messy black hair and brown eyes. I know it's him straight away, how could I have missed him? I walked straight past him! The woman uncufs them and they stand in a row with their heads bowed to stare at the floor, then follow her through the door with me following behind them.

I'm in Cole's memory!

Once the door is shut the boys are shown into a room where they sit on the floor with three girls, who also look severely underweight. There are two blondes and a red head, the red head has luminous green eyes and if it weren't for her sunken cheeks and blackened eye she would look stunning. She looks so familiar I can't help but stare at her as my mind tries to think who she reminds me of. She keeps her head down like the rest of them, except Cole who I notice out of the corner of my eye can't keep his eyes off her. He looks shocked and I guess the black eye is new. I stop staring as the sounds distract me.

The room is dark and grey and the magnificent fireplace looks almost more neglected than the kids do! I'm not sure if this is an orphanage or a children's prison! Spiders have nested in corners of the walls and as they sit on the floor rats are sniffing at their feet.

They are each given a plate of stale bread and a cup of water, I watch amazed as Cole rips the bread in half and gives it to the red head, who smiles at him lovingly as she pushes it back to him, instantly regretting the facial movement and wincing in pain. He has very strong feelings for her that is obvious, and she returns his feelings. I don't feel jealous for some reason even as strong as my feelings are for him, I am merely in awe. I feel a strange connection to her as though we have something in common.

The man and woman from before have retreated into a room to the side and with the door open I see the fire blasting heat for the two of them as they eat from full plates and drink from steaming cups. But these kids are left without warmth, and only bread and water. It's an insight into what made Cole a demon.

"Cole, are we getting out tonight?" another boy asks as he leans over the others and speaks so low he can barely be heard. Somehow I know his name is Ryan, as though I have met him before but don't remember.

"Yes, and we are taking Anne." he whispers back and the red head shoots her eyes at him, mouth open in shock.

"No way man, she will slow us down. I ain't getting caught for no one. I need your help and you need mine. She stays." The red head seems to nod her agreement with Ryan and I guess they have all been brought up here with the 'stick up for yourself and no one else' attitude.

"We are taking her Ryan, or I'm not going!" he warns his friend who groans with annoyance but backs down, using his arm to hide his plate from the eyes of one of the blonde girls.

"No, no way. I will stay here and do as I am told, and if you had any sense about you so would you!" she practically tells him off and I see the corner of his mouth raise in amusement, he really loves this girl and he must only be about 14 years old.

"I'll swing by after lights out, I can get you out of here Anne, I will get a job and we can be married before the year is out. I promise to make you happy." she smiles sadly and I can see that's what she wants but she doesn't want to risk hoping for it.

"If they catch you, then they will kill you. I don't want you dead Cole. I would rather not have you at all if it means you stay alive." The tears in her eyes are genuine, raw emotion, as she pleads with him to stay safe.

"Then I will die for you!"

I close my eyes as I try to take in what is happening and when I open them I see Cole pacing in a different room. He lays down on his bed, which creaks with the weight of him. A row of more creaky metal bed frames with thinnest mattresses ever known align one wall, with curtains surrounding them for privacy. It looks more like an old fashioned hospital. The door opens and the light turns off. Then after a few moments he is touched lightly by his friend Ryan on the shoulder. It's the signal that all is clear. He stands and begins quietly gathering his trousers and shoes having no other clothes or belongings.

The image fades and changes, he looks angry and scared pacing from one end of an empty bed to the other. I notice the others are in beds, and that they are girls.

Cole is in the girl's room to collect Anne and break her free of this place, but she isn't here. He is pacing franticly and I watch stunned as he actually looks frightened.

A scream sounds from somewhere in the building, a scream of terror and pain.

He bolts to the door and I follow, walking

behind him as he leaves the room. He takes a left turn and then two right turns. I lose track of where he is going but as more and more screams sound he gets faster and faster and harder to keep up with. He is calling her name as he goes. He opens a door and walks inside the room. The first thing he sees is the man from earlier stood by the fire, then his eyes shoot to Anne, sprawled out naked on the floor covered in blood and not moving. Blank eyes staring towards the ceiling.

"Ah, Cole it's about time you turned up. I am afraid Anne couldn't wait for you forever, although she did keep calling your name. But you never came for her." as he stands I see the scratches on his face, and he shakes and wobbles a little as he zips his trousers up. Cole can't stop staring at Anne, horror and pain etched on his face.

"No." the word escapes his mouth sounding agonisingly pained.

"You thought I couldn't hear you?" The man asks. "You were going to take away my Anne. You were going to take the one thing in this place that brings me joy. You were going to run away with her and marry her."

"You raped her."

"We had sex, regularly actually. She fucking loved it she did. My cock buried deep inside her while she pretended to be scared. They all fucking love to pretend they don't like it. But I know different. She fucking begged for it with her eyes all the time."

"You're a monster, you raped her and killed her!" Cole screams across the room.

"I taught her a lesson! And now I'm gonna do the same to you boy. You two tried to fuck me over, now I fucked that little shit over and now it's time to fuck you over. Bend over boy." His voice is so low it drips menace. Sickness hits my stomach watching this ugly confrontation and I move in front of Cole knowing it won't help. Tears streaming down my face. I stand before him horrified mumbling over and over "You won't harm him. You will not touch him." but when I turn to look back at Cole he just looks angry again, eyes moving from Anne to the man in front of the fire.

"You raped her. You hurt her. You killed her. My Anne." He whispers. His shock, pain and anger all role into one as he pounces at the man, jumping over the desk that stands between them and starts hitting him repeatedly. All of his emotions released at once as he takes in the fact that him escaping to marry his love has led to her being violently raped, beaten and murdered. The scene reminds me of the one I witnessed in the alleyway between James and Veronica when her fury built up so much she lashed out, defending herself.

He stands after seeing the man is unconscious, and he takes a sharp object from the desk, I think it is a letter opener. He pushes it straight into the man's chest watching mesmerised as blood seeps over his waist coat, seeping into his white shirt and spilling down onto the floor. The dumpy woman from earlier enters the room and screams in shock.

"You murderer!" she yells looking from one dead body to the other.

"No, he is the murderer and you aren't much better! I just gave him the justice he deserved. Better in fact, he deserved worse! And your time will come." he points his finger accusingly at her.

He stoops to cradle Anne, lifting her to his chest

and stroking and kissing her hair. His tears falling onto her face, sobbing uncontrollably. My tears falling onto the back of his head as I stand behind him wishing to hold him. He begins whispering her name as he rocks her lifeless body, treating her with as much care as a new mother would a new-born.

"We will see what the police have to say about this shall we." the woman turns to walk away and I hear the door close and lock behind her leaving him trapped. I know what will happen next. They will say Cole beat and raped Anne and murdered her, then murdered the man when he found them. I can't let that happen, and even as I think it I know it is ridiculous, there is nothing that I can do to stop it. I watch as Cole takes the knife out of the man's ribcage, and purposely runs it along his own wrists.

"I swear to find you were ever you go, I'm so sorry Anne please forgive me. I promise to protect you. We will be together again and I promise I will protect you. Nothing will ever hurt you again." he cries holding her face to his as he cries into her hair.

I come back to reality and find I am still sitting on the bench, the sky is getting darker telling me I have been sitting here for a few hours at least. I have to find Clara. She can help me figure this out. I try to stop feeling too emotional about watching Cole die but I can't stop the tears from falling. The shock of it all almost too much to handle.

I walk purposely back to the house but all the time I feel someone watching me, it has me turning back a few times and scanning for danger, but I just shrug it off as being too emotional and probably paranoid. I carry on back to Ally's house, where I find everyone sitting frustrated around the laptop.

"Oh thank god Violet, please tell me you have something to tell us? We found nothing!" Says Clara almost begging.

"Actually I do have something, tell me Clara what do you know about visions, and what are the chances I have had a life in between awakenings that I didn't remember until now." she looks confused as do the rest of the group and I sit down to explain the vision I saw from Cole's memory.

Chapter 11

"So, in the vision Anne looked incredibly familiar, I couldn't place my finger on it at the time but she looked exactly like I did in my human life, before I became a warrior. I didn't see what happened to her in Cole's memory but I KNOW what happened to her, it's like I remember being there all of a sudden. I remember her entire life. It has to be me, I was Anne. That's why as strong as my feelings are for Cole I didn't feel any jealousy what so ever for him loving her, because subconsciously I knew that she was me. But how is it possible? Why is it possible?" I ask the questions to the room as everyone stares at me blankly. "For crying out loud can't any of you explain any of this to me?" I beg.

"Violet, Cole is your purpose!" Clara says still stunned as George turns to stare at her, Damien nodding his agreement and entwining his fingers with hers.

"Sorry, what was that?" I ask completely bewildered.

"We have all been thinking Cole was your purpose but this proves it completely. Nature showed you that vision because it is time for you to remember, no doubt it wiped the memory until now because of all horrific the violence you had experienced. It was not vital for you to know about it until now, so nature's way of apologising to you for putting your soul through all of that was to help you forget until a time you could heal appropriately and do what must be done. But now it IS vital for you to remember." I continue to look blankly at her and she sighs.

"In that life nature knew those events would turn Cole into an evil demon bent on destroying the world in his revenge. But nature can not intervene so directly as to actually change anything that happened to him. Nature put your soul into Anne's body making Cole love YOU, and he still connects with your soul that's why you have been drawn to each other. Cole loves you."

"So this is all like some kind of wimpy love story, like in some book!" I say sarcastically to her and she looks about ready to slap me.

"Your purpose is to get him to stop his plan without actually destroying him. You have to make him CHOOSE to stop. You have to give him an alternative. Violet, Cole is your soul mate. Cole is your purpose. Cole is evil because of the things that happened to him in his human life, not because he was born evil. You have to HELP him, not fight him. This mission requires you to SAVE the bad guy!" Even as she says it I know she is right. "Nature chose your soul to inhabit the body of Anne back then so you could be here now. You and Cole are meant to be together. You are a vampire warrior, and yes you are in some wimpy love story. Next you will be wearing dresses and pretty shoes and whistling with an apron tied around your waist making homemade bread."

"Someone's been watching too much television." laughs Ally.

"I like the cooking channel, so what!" Defends Clara.

"That's a lot to take in!" Says Ally turning back to me.

"Nature sucks." I mumble much like a child having a tantrum.

"Yeah, we know." Everyone agrees.

"So you found nothing on how to find angels?" I ask hesitantly, knowing time is running out.

"Nope." Answers Ally from across the breakfast bar, laptop closed in front of her signalling they gave up with it.

"We found nothing on finding angels, seeing angels or going to the realm of the angels. The search for killing them was more successful than this!" Clara is getting frustrated and I don't blame her. We are in a race to save the souls of two innocent children and we are most definitely not in the lead.

"What if we are thinking about this all wrong? I know it's not ideal but what if we won't be able to find the angels until they are already in this realm. Once they are here they will be as obvious as any other girl or boy."

Her words sound like they make sense, but it means letting him kidnap the souls. Can we really just sit back and let him take them?

"The magical change will be obvious to all magical souls, no doubt it will awake many old souls near them and that alone will be enough of a change to draw us to them. I don't like the idea of Cole luring innocents to this world either guys but the longer we sit here and look up how to find them the more chance there is that he will do it while we are unprepared. Maybe we should just go out there and look for Cole, try to find his base or whatever and we could stop him before he starts." Alliyana's words pull on all our heart strings and we know we need to get out there looking for Cole.

"Thank you Ally, looks like we might be in need of your wisdom as well as your home." I say and hug her. She smiles and hugs me back.

"You have to find Cole, then hopefully you can reach out to his soul and change his intentions *before* he kidnaps the angels." Clara says and throws a jacket at Ally. "You are going to have to come with us, you will have bonds with more mermaid souls than we do meaning more chance of finding some information. And we need all the help we can get." She says pushing her out of the door.

We all walk outside together as a group, sending out our senses for changes in the atmosphere, but we pick up on nothing. Just a minor soul awakening here or there which is most likely to be from other warriors. We begin by walking in any direction and scanning for souls to awaken and question.

Cole must be blocking our bond, no matter how often I sense for him I can't feel him. I pick up on a slight feeling of loneliness now and then, or become irritated suddenly and believe I am sensing his feelings, but no clue to his position or even a pull in his direction.

I sense a soul nearby and wince, but I know this is too important an opportunity to let it pass. An old friend is living close by and I believe she can help, I just have to hope she isn't too angry at me for killing her. Looking into Veronica's memories I see the legend that has been built up over the many years and almost laugh out loud. You would know her as Medusa, but I know her as Jen.

I find the house very easily, much like I did Ally's, and stand for a moment before knocking. You see legend says it was Perseus who beheaded Medusa, which in a way is true. I did indeed take his body and slay her. But she was overcome with power and at the very end she knew it was the only way she could escape the darkness that was consuming her.

Jen was the only mortal out of her and her three sisters, yet she was absolutely beautiful. Her long dark hair always looked beautiful and her body was the dream of all men that saw her, she was able to get anything and everything she wished for just by looking at men and batting her eyelids. But the expectations of her family were ludicrously high. The poor girl just wanted to be normal, but they had it in their minds she was destined for greatness, to be a goddess, and constantly made her feel inadequate. The darkness inside her fed off these emotions and she found herself wanting to make her family happy more than anything. She was given the name Medusa to strike fear in the hearts of other humans.

To explain it better think of her as two different people, Medusa was the name of the darkness and Jen was the name of the woman. Jen was madly in love with Perseus and wanted desperately to lead a normal life, get married and have children. But Medusa saw Perseus as a distraction, he was getting in the way of her plans. It was Medusa who killed Perseus and left Jen weeping for him. I took over Perseus's body in order to reach Jen after she had let the darkness consume her. The mirrored shield was to distract Medusa, letting me get close and personal with Jen, and while in her lover's body I killed her.

I hope she has forgiven me, if memory serves me correctly which it always has before Jen knew magic at such a high level that she knew how to reach the world of the angels, which was why she needed to be destroyed at that time. With darkness consuming her, making her more and more powerful who knows what havoc could have been caused.

When the door opens I see a tall woman with

long blonde hair, and beautifully striking blue eyes. Again I see the look of familiarity cross her face and I send my soul to retrieve hers, but I find someone else has already beaten me to it.

"Well I never." she says after a few moments.

"Hello Jen, it's been a while."

"I didn't think I would see you again." She stands aside and lets me in the house. No smile, no hug, barely any recollection at all, and follows me down the hallway.

"Jen, we need your help." I notice a slight look of panic in her eyes but she quickly recomposes herself and stares at me.

"I haven't heard anything Violet, I swear." She seems rather uncomfortable and I can't help but pick up on the little things. Her breathing is harsh and there are beads of sweat on her fore head. She looks kind of terrified.

"Jen, what's wrong?" I ask and her eyes shoot to mine.

"Nothing. Why?" she laughs but it doesn't reach her eyes. She drops the smile and her eyes shoot up, showing me that whatever she is afraid of is upstairs. When she looks back to me she is pleading for me not to go on. She is actually afraid of something. Or someone?

"Oh my, look Jen what happened in the past is in the past. There is no reason to fear me. I don't want to hurt you." I say loudly so whoever it is does not suspect anything. "Jeez calm down will you, I only wanted some information and you don't have any. Now put the kettle on and make yourself a nice cup of tea to calm your nerves, we have some catching up to do!" she looks confused as I pick up a large knife from the draining board, but she flicks the kettle on anyway. I use the sound of it boiling to mask my steps through the house as I start looking around. Jen looks like she is about to collapse with fear and keeps trying to motion me out of the house.

I creep up the stairs and find myself looking into a bathroom, I turn at the top and listen to the sounds behind the doors. As I get to the first door and press my ear against it the door at the end of the corridor opens. And there stands Cole watching me.

"I wondered how long it would take for you to catch up. Pretty clever aren't we angel?" he smiles and somehow it's both evil and sweet.

"Well I don't mean to be rude darling but 'clever' would be NOT falling for the enemy." I point out with my own smile cursing myself for feeling such a rush to see him. His eyes burn into mine for a moment with a motive all too clear as his gaze eventually travels over the rest of my body before he turns and vanishes back into the room. I know he is gone yet I can't stop my legs taking me to the doorway anyway. I stand and search for him in the darkness, but he is already gone.

I pick up on the feeling of loneliness, both mine and his mingling together. I don't know if it's that he can't hide his emotions from me or just that he doesn't want to, but it makes me shuffle down to my knees and lean against the doorway, my head resting on the cold hard wood of the frame, cheeks wet from the crying I promised myself I wouldn't do any more.

"Well he is gone, and I don't think he will be coming back." I tell Jen when I get back downstairs, she hadn't even tried to run. What's the point against a demon? "What did he do to you?" her hands go up to the sides of her head as she closes her eyes looking in the midst of a full blown panic attack, her breathing is quick and yet it looks like she can't get enough air in her lungs.

"He wanted to know a spell. One for crossing realms, something about angels? I didn't give him the spell I couldn't. But he has Pete and I don't know what he will do to him." She is physically shaking and pacing around the room.

"Pete who?" I ask and she gives me a look that says I asked the wrong question.

"Pete, Perseus. My love!" she answers.

"Oh wow, you found each other again?" I say smiling, momentarily forgetting everything else.

"We did!" she yells. "But now that demon has him. He wants me to tell him the spell or he is going to kill him. Violet what am I going to do?" I rub her shoulders trying to calm her down but it doesn't work, she falls apart in front of me. The woman that was once so consumed by evil she would kill people just for looking at her is now on her knees in front of me, begging for help and snot crying into her hands. "He could be torturing him right now and all I can do is sit here and wait for the demon to show up, and even then I don't know if Pete's safe." She sobs.

"Jen, I'm gonna do my best to bring him down I swear it. But you have to help me. I need your help more than anybody else's right now." she looks up at me.

"Violet I can't help you, I don't know where he is or what he wants or anything, I only know he wants the spell for crossing realms, that is all." she answers me looking angry at herself.

"No no I don't mean like that. Jen do you remember when the darkness had you, and there was only one way out of it?" she looks up at me frightened for a whole new reason. "The demon,

Cole, is getting very close to being the same. I know him, he isn't evil. Something happened in his life and when he died darkness offered his soul revenge on those that hurt him. And he accepted. That's how he became a demon, and the more darkness grabs him the more powerful he becomes. I need to defeat this darkness without defeating Cole. Do you understand me?" she nods, her sobbing ceased for now as she stands.

"What do you need?" she whispers.

"Information. Not about the demon or even the spell. Right now I need information on you. More specifically you're past. How can we get past the darkness?" I ask her and she closes her eyes looking apprehensive. I can tell she doesn't want to revisit her past but this is the only way we can save Pete.

"He will go mad, eventually all that will matter is getting what he wants the most. Lives will be lost and he won't even notice. That's the worse stage, when killing becomes as normal as putting milk on your cereal. The power won't be enough and he will constantly want more, it's a drug." She sits on the sofa after leading me to the living room and she just stares at the floor with her hands in her knee. "Perseus was the only person that could really reach me, it was like I was in a cage in my own mind. But I didn't want to be free. Freedom meant responsibility and that meant facing my own guilt. After the first few people I decided to let darkness take over so I wouldn't feel the pain that I had caused. It's always there even now, begging me to let it in again, but I can't. Perseus was my soul mate and I killed him. It wasn't meant to be him he just got in the way. It was straight after I killed him that you killed me. To destroy the darkness before it destroyed the world." she is crying silently, tears spilling down her face and crashing to the carpet.

"How can I defeat the darkness?" I ask her.

"You have to reach the soul. You love him, yes?" she asks looking at me and the only answer I can give her is a quick nod of my head.

"Then tell him you love HIM. You need his soul, not his powers. Reach out to his soul and let him know whatever he is escaping he can face with you at his side."

"Jen, I need you to tap into your power and tell me the spell for crossing realms. Hopefully I can stop him hurting the souls of some angels."

"I can't, if I tap into my power darkness will know. What if it takes me again? What if I let it?" she sobs and I put my hand on her shoulder.

"You won't, just keep thinking about Pete. And about how much he needs you." the thought seems to bring her back to reality.

"Your right, I'll do it."

Chapter 12

It is truly amazing what we will sacrifice for love, Jen is going to face darkness again in order to save Pete and I am planning to cross realms to save Cole. He needs rescuing from the darkness or he will be lost forever. We walk towards the destination I feel Alliyana and I sense another old soul. When I reach the house she is just leaving, she shakes her head and shrugs her shoulders when she spots us and I assume that means she didn't get any information.

"Nothing, sorry Violet." she says as she closes the gate behind her to join us on the street. I smile and touch her arm to let her know it's OK.

"This is Jen, Jen this is my good friend Ally." she smiles at Ally and shakes her hand.

"It's nice to meet you Ally, I don't think I have ever met a mermaid before." her smile widens as Ally's eyes light up.

"Oh my, you're Medusa!" she breaths. "I have read up all about your story, a lot of it seems fictional but I would love to hear the truth."

"I think we should get along just fine." Jen giggles and I see her appreciation of Ally, well she did just figure out that Jen was Medusa from a handshake!

I scan for the others while the two get to know each other and I sense George is the closest, so I begin walking with Jen and Alliyana following behind me. I need the gang together so we can do a group cast, find Jen's powers, find the spell and perform it, sending me to the realm of the angels to look for Cole. I sense George with another old soul and prey he managed to find something to help us.

When we arrive at the house I knock on the door, a man answers and lets us in without asking any questions at all. I sense an old soul but again this is a soul I don't know. Something isn't right and I feel my entire body go on instant alert.

I walk into the house and find George in the living room, he seems fine at a first glance but a closer inspection reveals he looks almost ashamed.

"Violet, we have a problem." he says and nods towards a doorway at the other side of the room, in which stands Brian.

"Brian, what is the meaning of this?" I say as I notice his evil looking smile. Why didn't I sense him?

"Well, talk of the devil. I knew she would come looking for you at some point." he says amused and shoots George an *I told you so* expression. "We were just discussing you, weren't we?"

"Brian remember who I am, and what I can do. And remember I am already pissed at you." I warn him with my voice cold as ice.

"Oh don't worry Violet I remember exactly who you are, the thing is I am not quite the same person any more. I have switched sides, joined with someone that will appreciate me, and understand me. Someone that shares the power and glory. Someone that won't lead me on!" he spits at me.

"Brian, I never lead you on. I told you from day one that I was not interested. I have never been interested in you like that. This jealousy act has gone far enough, you need to grow up and realise the seriousness of the situation. The world is in danger for crying out loud that's a little bigger than your stupid pride. Now get out and let us get on with our purposes or I swear I will make you very sorry indeed!"

"Now, now Violet, you wouldn't want to make me angry." before I know it he is behind me with my arms twisted behind my back. "Would you?" And realisation hits me like a brick in the face. *He isn't a warrior any more, he is a demon!*

"How is this possible?" I ask struggling to break free.

"I changed my mind about protecting the balance, I have been a good boy for centuries and I never got anything in return. An evil demon comes along and you're weak at the knees! That tells me you like bad boys, a bit of danger turns you on. So here I am, all ready for you."

"But how?" I ask shocked and angry.

"By simply giving myself to another, these demons have a lot of power you know. Now come, there's something I have been desperate to do to you for a very long time." His voice becomes harsh as he starts pushing me forwards towards the stairs. The others in the room start to jump up to help but all at once they freeze, Brian is already more powerful than I am.

He starts to push me upstairs, and I feel an anger so overpowering I find myself letting him take me upstairs, but I stop when we reach the top and throw myself down them to escape him. I tumble to the bottom breaking an elbow that heals within seconds. I vaguely hear a sound of disgust from behind me before my entire body stops, my nose is an inch off the carpet. I have frozen mid-air before hitting the bottom.

"Tut, tut." I hear from somewhere above me and my body starts moving on its own. I'm stood up, walking up the stairs. *He is controlling me!* I feel the fear building and building, replacing my anger almost completely. I walk into a room and lay down on the bed staring at the ceiling while in my head screeching at him not to touch me. Memories of Anne and Veronica flood my mind, of the abuse they suffered. This is worse, this is abuse from a demon. He shuts the door and turns around to face me.

"That's a good girl, you know you want this. You know all along this is exactly what you wanted. You need a man that will just take what he wants. And not that I know that, I can be that man. I can forgive you and Cole, I'm not saying I'm not angry." he sits on the bed beside me and the entire atmosphere in the room is icy. "I'm going to take this real slow so you can thoroughly enjoy everything." His hand is on my waist and moving my top up over my stomach, I wish I could spit in his face but I can't move. The anger inside me bubbles and threatens to explode but the worse thing of all is what can I do if it does explode? All I can do is lay here. His hand is on my breast, grabbing and playing roughly and I wish I could at least close my eyes, but he keeps them open and staring at him. He is making me watch him abuse me.

"That feels great baby, I love it rough." He forces words out of my mouth and I wish I could kick him where it hurts. I feel my face smiling as I start to moan as though I'm enjoying this torture.

"That's right baby you do, and things are going to get a whole lot rougher than you have ever known. I'm gonna rock your world." He leans down and bites my nipple, my mind screams in pain as I feel him draw blood. I feel the warmth start in my toes, and after a few seconds of white hot rage burning up inside me I find I have control of my body again. I bring my first up, connecting with Brian's jaw with such impact it shatters leaving him howling. Before it has had time to heal I grab him by his balls and hoist him off the bed, if he hadn't been a demon it would have killed him. He lands on ground on one knee clearly in agony, but still aware of what is going on. He holds his hand up as though to tell me to stop and my body freezes again. I managed to catch him by surprise last time, but now he isn't going to take that chance. He flings me backwards and pins me against the wall with his powers.

I am bound by an invisible force with my hands at my sides, as though strapped to the wall. Brian stands and spits blood on the carpet while his body finishes healing. As he stares at me his nose crinkles with hate and disgust, he brushes the back of his sleeve across his face to wipe away some of the excess. He takes a step towards me and looks me up and down before unbuttoning his jeans. I can see the excitement in his eyes and I scream inside for help. The thought of Brian taking what he wants makes me feel physically ill and if I could I know I would be shaking with fear.

A noise downstairs catches my attention, but Brian is so focused on seeking the warmth of my body that he quickly pulls his top over his head and discards it across the room, stepping out of his trousers and making his way towards me.

"Well. I think you need to learn a lesson in respect. And I'm just the person to do it." His fist slams into the side of my face while his free hand grabs my thighs, pulling them apart while they stick like Velcro to the wall behind me.

Before I know what is happening the door

bursts open, splinters flying all over the room. I can't move my head at all but I see Cole standing behind Brian taking in the scene, looking from my blooded and broken face to Brian in his just his shorts, and I thank nature for sending him to me. He grabs Brian's shoulders from behind and in a strange move lifts him from the ground to slam him back down, it clearly affects his entire body and even his eyes seem to roll in his head looking for balance.

I fall to the ground when the invisible ties dissipate and I take it upon myself to cower in a corner. I don't cower from them, nor from the scene, instead I cower from what would have happened next. The fear that had me is hard to shake and I can't stop my head from playing the entire ugly scene in my head. The images of Brian raping me and overpowering me, I take advantage of my body being my own and I scream out loud. I stand up just as Cole takes hold of Brian and before he can stun him again, thrust my hand into his chest.

I hadn't even noticed the burning sensations that time, all I knew was that my hand inside Brian's chest holding his heart felt warm and delicious. Brian was so scared he had tears in his eyes as I held in my hand his very life. Cole had backed off looking afraid but I was too far gone to care or even notice. The ecstasy had taken over. I knew this was a risk when using my full powers, it feels so good I don't want to be tempted yet sometimes I can't control the fury. It builds up and feeds something inside me, something I had wanted to remain hidden.

"I guess you worked out your anger problems." Brian's voice was broken, but his eyes were looking deep into mine with envy. My fingers clenched and tightened, Brian writhed in agony until finally I ripped his heart out of his chest cavity and threw it onto the floor.

"You're a goddess!" Cole whispered from across the room, and without another word he marched straight towards me and held me safely in his arms. His lips crashed onto mine as his hands worked to stroke every inch of me protectively. The burning feeling faded and I was left a broken woman hiding in his embrace. I began to cry as he slid to the floor kneeling with me, surrounded by him like a safety blanket murmuring shushing sounds and telling me I will be ok.

"I'm not a goddess." I whimper eventually, sniffling back tears and trying to remind myself that I'm stronger than this. He just continues to hold me.

"You are a goddess to me Violet."

I don't know how long we sat cuddling and connecting emotionally, but eventually he kissed the top of my head and pulled back. The others from downstairs walked slowly up the stairs and into the room. They saw me sitting in a puddle of blood and tears, Cole kissing me and Brian's dead body. Then Cole disappeared out of the window.

"Violet, how he did that?" asks George looking over Brian's body as though he might jump up at any minute.

"He turned himself over to darkness." I whisper still gazing out of the window after Cole. Jen comes to me and without saying a word starts to adjust my clothing, clearing up the mess that Brian left by making me look and feel presentable. When she washes the blood off I feel like crying all over again as relief comes to me in waves.

"What was Cole doing here?"
"He saved me."

Chapter 13

"We need to find the others, then we can all do a group casting and get Jen's powers back. Hopefully she can find the spell for crossing realms, I can go and save these angels and at the same time hopefully save Cole from himself." I sense Clara and Damien together as I knew they would be, and I 'call' them to me. I can send out a sort of emotion that nudges them into wanting to come to me. They will wrap up whatever they are doing, send out their senses to search for me and come to us that way. I don't really like using that power, I always feel like my manipulation of their minds is a sort of intrusion. Right now whether I like it or not I need them here ASAP and that means doing things that I don't really like.

While we wait for the last two members of the group I get acquainted with George's friend Vincent, who actually turns out to be the reincarnated soul of Leonardo Da Vinci himself. Only after I find that out do I notice the art work on the walls, scrunched up paint tubes, half-finished canvases, models, writing pens, ruffled up papers and god only knows what else cluttering every work surface around the place. To anyone else this place would look a mess, but to a great creator like him it was a heaven bursting with art and possibilities. You could practically hear his pride as he spoke of his work, which is really the sign of a true artist. Anyone can paint a yellow line on a blue background which I see is todays rendition of artwork, but rarely is it seen that an artist can put all of his emotion, all of his… everything! Into his work.

After a brief, and rather uncomfortable introduction we sit down and begin discussing casting a circle to search for Jen's power. It will take a lot of concentration, so I hope I can keep my mind off Cole for a short while, my hands shake slightly with worry that he might be too far gone with darkness for me to help him. I hope I don't have to kill him the way I killed Jen all that time ago.

We sit in a circle on the floor so we can all see each other and let our energies flood from ourselves and accept the energy of the group. We need to learn how be one person, while still being many, and all in a matter of minutes where others have years. I fear we may be asking too much yet one by one the group starts to come under a sort of trance, instant relaxation hits as they force every thought out of their head. Of course it isn't that simple for me, while everyone in the group is thinking of nothing and enjoying the freedom it brings I am imagining killing Cole and trying to not get too worked up as the images refuse to leave my mind.

When Clara and Damien arrive we are all still sat in a circle, me still trying to relax and sink into a deep and unemotional state of mind, getting ready to begin the task ahead. What I love the absolute most about these guys is they can walk into a room and find everyone on the carpet in a circle, and they join in without hesitation or question, no wasting time with what can always be explained later. I look around the group and take pride in knowing these amazing souls trust me completely, I just wish I could trust myself as much as they do. I decided that they deserve for me to really sort myself out and I do my best to push all thoughts of Cole from my mind and concentrate whole heartedly on the group.

"Does everyone know what they need to be doing?" Jen asks and everyone nods at her waiting for the signal. "Just listen to the sound of my voice, ignore the person beside you breathing heavily, ignore the sound of someone swallowing loudly across from you, they are all sounds of nature. Don't let them distract you."

When we are all seated and ready Jen closes her eyes, her voice falling on the group and instantly creating an atmosphere fit for meditation. She tells us to focus on her spirit and imagine in our minds a large box filled with all different kinds of items. We have already decided on a specific item to use as a visionary tool to symbolize her power, a torch. Something that gives light. We need to focus in our minds and imagine we are searching through this large box for the torch. As is obvious the torch symbolises Jen's power. We cannot simply imagine finding the torch and all is well, we have to send out a positive energy that is searching to help Jen.

She starts humming deeply across the room and her melodious voice falls on our ears like the delicate humming of a bee murmuring words in her language as we strain to hear her perfect song, spoken in a language too long forgotten as a smile spreads on my face from the sheer beauty of it. The entrancing sound of old age and magic having me feeling almost at home and human again, ironic really that it takes being reminded of magic to remember when I was a human. Her song removes any doubt from the entire group and I feel everyone connect and strengthen from it.

I envision a large box that looks like a treasure chest, with bits of elegant shimmery fabric and gold necklaces spilling out. In my mind I start sifting through the box looking for the torch. I try really hard to keep myself from thinking about Cole but it's difficult, especially since all of this is to save him from himself and stop him becoming completely evil.

The box swims out of view after a few minutes searching, at first I think I'm about to see the torch and start to think we have done it. But I hear a voice that snaps my eyes open to see I am surrounded by fog, I can hear Cole! But where is he? I turn my head searching for him but all I see is endless mist clouding my view. I hear his voice again, and I move blindly towards it eventually losing the fog and stepping into what looks like a children's playground.

I see two little girls, one sat on a chair idly fiddling with the hem of her dress and kicking her feet, the other skipping happily almost in slow motion as though the fluorescent rainbow coloured rope is letting her win. They have the most beautiful dresses and shoes matching in everything but the colour. One is wearing a lilac dress and shoes with a green sash and diamonds in her pumps, and the other is wearing a green dress and shoes with lilac sash and diamonds. White knee socks with a floral lace pattern stitched in silver around the tops. Both girls have stunning deep blue eyes, cute round button noses and long blonde curly hair in perfectly styled ringlets slinking past their shoulders, they look as though they will never be able to get messy or crumpled. They sing nursery rhymes together in perfect unison, it's the usual cliché for most horror films these days and yet everything about these girls is so perfectly wonderful I want to hold their hands and play with them and make the smile. I feel instantly protective.

"Hello there girls." Cole appears bathed in a white light, wearing white trousers and a white polo neck sweater and of course white lace up shoes. He leans down on one knee to get to their level, and grins the most amazing smile ever while looking from one to the other, eyes filled with nothing but serenity yet I know behind them is a spell to hide his deception. "My name is Cole, I'm your protector."

"I am Isabelle." Says the girl with the lilac dress, her voice is pure silk and her manners are impeccable. "My sister is Bella." The girl with the skipping rope smiles and courtesy's as though in the presence of a king, Cole chuckles and rubs her cheek gently, almost lovingly with the back of his hand as bile starts to work its way up my throat. I run forward and try to take their hands to pull them away from him, but I go straight through them as though I am a ghost.

"Well girls I am here to tell you it is time for you to move on."

"Move on to where?" the girls ask together, I can't stop myself from crying and yet again murmuring to myself the one word repeatedly *no, no, no, no!* But nobody hears or sees me, because I aren't really there. Cole has passed realms which leaves him vulnerable, he is letting me in through our bond whether he wants to or not. I feel physically sick thinking that I could love a man capable of such an evil, devious act. In this moment I know if my choice was to kill him I would. If only to get him away from those girls.

"To move on to your next life." He answers warmly.

"Will we still be together?"

"Of course you will." He has no right to promise something he can't guarantee, and I have to look him square in the eye even if he can't hear or see me.

"I will kill you if you hurt them Cole." I say out loud to him, and one of the girls takes a step away from him turning around as though she heard me. "Yes, Isabella listen to me. You must not go with him!" I plead praying I am right.

"Who is that?" she asks looking around for the voice, alerting Cole instantly.

"We must go, evil is breaking through!" He holds his hands out for the girls to take, and much to my own despair they do.

The scene is like something out of a corny film, the man in white leading the two angels to a new life as they disappear in to the distance all happy and giddy. Only when I come around from the vision I am screaming and crying, and curled up on the floor shaking from the horror. I feel a hand on my cold clammy forehead and look up to see George eyeing me with worry.

"Cole has taken the girls." I whisper and the entire room erupts around me.

Chapter 14

"Violet, what did you see?" asks Damien clearly shaken up by the intensity of my emotions.

"No time for details!" I shout at them. "He has the girls. We have to track him down NOW. Move!" Cole has the souls of two girls trapped here, where he will frighten them into believing they are only safe if they stay with him. And then get them to hand over their power. Who knows what he will do to them next.

We run for hours without stopping, all of us sensing where the souls are. Alliyana and Jen were left behind as they are still human in their bodies, they cannot run as fast nor for as long as we can. The spell to enchant himself into their world must have blocked the powers he was using to block me, that's why I could see it all happening. He was in a world so powerfully enhanced the bond between us was strengthened for a short while at the same time he was weakened. I cringe as I recall the way he lured the girls away from safety, and I almost choke on tears to think what he could be doing to them or telling them right now. The only comfort I find is knowing that the power stones have to be given wilfully and for that he must earn their trust completely.

We all stop outside an old decrepit building, feeling the magic as a barrier. It's not a barrier that we can't cross, but it's one that we don't want to. The magic is so power full it deflects anybody going near it. Anybody that doesn't know what is inside will simply walk away from the building.

But we do know what is inside. Slowly we all walk forward as one towards the flimsy looking building, as I open the doors it looks like an abandoned barn complete with a creaky door and bits of ceiling covering the floor. I sense something not quite right and as I look harder the enchantment lifts, it was disguised as a barn at a glance to anyone who made it past the barrier, and only when taking a closer look does the building become clearer. Not a barn but it still looks abandoned. We open the door that looks like it's about to fall off anyway and enter a side hallway. After wandering down corridor after corridor we start to see this place, it looks like an old school. Classrooms with pictures on the doors and notice boards on the walls. The enchantment must still be wearing off as we didn't notice the colours before. Of course he took them to a school, it's bright and colourful and welcoming to kids. The really worrying thing is what he did to everyone else that should be here right now.

We hear kids playing, laughing and yelling, we follow the noise to what looks like a cafeteria. The girls sit throwing peas at each other and laughing loudly. I sense him, Cole. And I know he senses me to.

"He knows we are here." I whisper, not wanting to disturb the girls from playing as a door opens from the other end and he appears. The noise disturbs the girls and they turn to look at him, their instant smiles for him make me feel sick. He has twisted their minds, to these girls he is a magnificent hero for keeping them safe.

"Cole!" they screech and run to him, throwing their arms around him as though they haven't seen him for a long time. "We thought you were too busy to play!"

"Now girls, I have some information and you have to listen to me very carefully. The evil that came for you in your realm is here now. It's what is stopping you from being reborn into your new lives. I need to destroy it so you can be safe." The girls cower to him.

"Stop." I say. Not too loud to scare the girls but loudly enough for him to hear me. He stands up from hugging the girls, staring at me with longing and sadness. I feel it, I know he has let his guard down. The girls panic and hide behind him, making me feel sick to my stomach and yet I feel Clara bound her way over to my side without taking her eyes off them.

"Cole you don't have to do this." I say, begging him to listen.

"Don't talk to me like a child, like a lunatic with a gun. Violet this is not about us this is about something higher than that. You have no idea what I am doing or what I am doing it for so do not patronise me!" he shouts, even the girls recoil afraid and he instantly puts his arms around their shoulders remembering he needs them to trust him. "It's bad enough you turn up and make me doubt myself, now you turn up and try to take these girls?" he is turning the situation around, making me sound like I want to take them away from him out of spite. He tries to block his emotions but I feel how confused he is. How jumbled the world is in his eyes right now.

"What would Anne think to your revenge?" Cole freezes.

"How do you know about Anne?"

"I know everything Cole, I was there. That's why we are so connected now, that's why we can't explain how we feel for each other. I am Anne." I whisper, pleading him to believe me as his eyes search mine.

"It can't be. You can't be!"

"I know, but I am."

"Anne?" his mouth moves but no sound comes out. I nod, all the tears in the world flooding our faces and I even feel the emotion radiating from the vampires behind me. The two girls look confused and kind of uncomfortable and move out of Cole's arms to stand behind him again. He walks towards me and takes my head with his hands.

"How could this be?" he asks, and I can do nothing but stare into his eyes. He kisses me hard, and when he is done his forehead rests on mine. A trait I have come to love about him.

"This is fate, this is love. This is how it should be, right here like this. Oh Anne, Violet. The world is our oyster, rule it with me. You can join me, take over with me. I love you, I always loved you. When I was given the choice to move on I said no, I wandered the earth lifeless for centuries before I gained my power, I thought of nothing but you, of what I caused. I grew strong loving the memory of you, you were given to me and snatched away. Now we will be together forever. Now we are in charge, we make our own destiny's because we will rule everything!" even though he is whispering I feel the harshness to his voice, and it makes me step back from him. The tears are for a new reason now and he watches me puzzled as I shake my head.

"No Cole. Not like this. You have to stop this insane plan for revenge or you will destroy everything. There will be nothing left to rule! These angels don't belong here. You have to let them go." I say flatly, and his eye brows raise. His voice booms through the cafeteria.

"It is not your place to tell me what to do. Nobody tells me what to do. I will rule the world, I will make my own destiny. I will do as I please to whom I please WHEN I please!" he shouts, voice amplified with power as it bounces from every surface and hits us again and again, the girls jump in fear, they turn to run but he grabs them by an arm each.

"You will give me your powers and you will do it now or..." he doesn't get to finish his sentence. Clara is stood in front of him, shocking him into letting go of the girls by punching him in his stomach causing him to double over in pain and surprise. She pushes the girls over towards Damien and he picks them up and gets them out of there, George following close behind to help as planned.

"Enough!" says Cole aggressively and he takes Clara by the throat, although she still hits and kicks as she doesn't need to breathe so strangling is a little pointless. She is giving time to Damien and George to get the girls far away, she knows he will probably kill her but she doesn't care. I step in front of him and kiss him passionately, and he lets go of Clara who runs straight after George and Damien.

His hands are on my face and I feel his desperation. Not for me but for justice. He needs to punish the world for what happened, he has lost all compassion over the years. The need to make things even gone and replaced with the need to destroy.

"We shall do it together, you will join me now. Together we will find a new way to rule all, make our own destiny, and never let anyone be in charge of us again. We will destroy anything that stands in our way. Now the world is OUR orphanage Anne. WE are in control." he kisses me again and although I know why he is how he is, and I understand why he needs the control, I still can't be with him. I am a creature that destroys the threats and while he is working with darkness he is still a threat.

"Oh Cole, can't it just be enough for you that I am here now, with you?" I ask already knowing the answer.

"Of course it isn't enough, I will make sure nobody takes you away from me again. I am in control now, nobody will hurt you or take you from me Anne. My love, I didn't look out for you before but now I am. You WILL rule with me." he is warning me now and I know it is time to go.

I turn and walk away listening to him call me back, the threatening tone in his voice as he warns me using only my name. He begins running, and I run quicker than I have ever ran in any of my awakenings. I think nature must have helped push me on, he doesn't catch up to me. When I reach the others they have already put the angels back in their world with the help of their power stones and explained to them that they must NEVER give them up to anybody. We cannot cross with them so we have to just assume they made it home safely. I understand Clara gave them a very firm lecture on trusting strangers, and how grownups shouldn't be near them in their realm so they can't trust anyone not one little bit. Which is kind of ironic as it was a grown up telling them that.

We make our way back to Alliyana's house, unsure of what happens now. Not knowing what we must do as the angels have been returned so that threat has been vanquished yet here we still stand.

We have not defeated Cole, we haven't returned

to nature and he is still adamant on ruling the world. This isn't going to be good but all we can do is sit back and wait for a sign. Something to tell us what to do. A nudge in the right direction.

Chapter 15

We wait around for days but nothing happens. It's weird not having anything to do, we don't sleep so we can't even escape for a while. It's as though we are stuck in limbo. Nothing happens and nothing is shown to us. We walk around Alliyana's house hoping for something to be shown to us and waiting to find out what we must do.

It was Friday when we freed the angels, now it is Monday and we still have no clue what we are even doing here still. We spent the entire weekend searching, scanning, waking souls, running, meditating and getting nothing back at all. Obviously Cole is still adamant on ruling the world otherwise we would be back within nature now.

Ally walks in from work a little earlier than she told us to expect her and straight away Clara is in the kitchen to start cooking for her, she had hoped to have a meal waiting for her return.

"I wouldn't bother with that Clara but thank you anyway, I have some bad news. It looks like we were looking in all the wrong places." she whispers looking at us all, eyes almost guilty as though it was her fault and she should have known better. We watch as she walks out of the room and we hear her turn on the television. We follow her into the living room where she is sitting on the sofa with her head in her hands, the news channel on with sirens blaring and we listen to what the pretty woman with bags underneath her eyes is saying.

"The young children have been trapped in the school since Friday, nobody knows how many will

survive. All we know is that whatever caused the school to bury itself is no doubt also to blame for the fires, floods and other catastrophes to happen in this small town. What could possibly cause so much chaos and damage in the space of only a few days? We have no answers. A bigger mystery is how the school has managed to bury itself in pristine condition, it is simply as though the ground opened up and something slotted the entire building into place. The workers here as you see are fighting desperately to cut through the rock to reach the schools entrance but none of their drills can even make a dint in the hardened substance, another option is to cut a whole out of the ceiling from one of the air ducts but with no way of knowing who is underneath the ceiling this being classed as the 'last minute' plan, which I'm now being told will be tomorrow, according to the supplies the school should have, they would be running out of food and water today."

I stop listening, too shocked to continue. I hadn't noticed other children in the school on Friday but perhaps that was all him, he must have cloaked us from the other children and vice versa. We were all so worked up about getting the angel girls out of the school we didn't even stop to figure out what he had done to everyone else. I remember thinking about it while inside the school, but I didn't do anything about it.

"I have to go." I say to the group of warriors watching the television with horror and they all nod silently knowing there is nothing they can say, clearly understanding that I do indeed HAVE to go. For good. For the safety of the children in that school and the rest of the town.

AWAKE AGAIN

I stand and run out of the house with my emotions fighting against each other. Every thought in my head conflicting another, I don't particularly want to see Cole again but I have to save those kids. As I run, nature is back pushing me on faster and faster. As I start to get close to the school I see crowds of people with shovels and trays of drinks or sandwiches. Most of the people in the crowd are hurrying with their lunch so they can keep on digging, dread etched on their faces, they look like they haven't slept in days and I know they probably haven't. Others are clearly working through lunch and not for the first time as their weakened arms barely even connect with the rock.

These are the parents of the children trapped inside. The mothers walking around with a zombie look on their faces and trays in their hands, one woman is walking around with an empty tray and still offering sandwiches, her grief making her body work on auto pilot so much she hasn't yet noticed and the others barely having the heart to tell her. They all work endlessly needing something to take their minds off where their babies are. I walk forward pushing past crowds of onlookers talking and begging for encouragement until I reach a huge hole in the ground. Buried about thirty feet down is the school building. It was one of those concrete and tar roofs, not tiled. Which means they would have to cut a chunk out to get inside and it would fall into the class room beneath, if anyone was under it they would most definitely not survive.

I, however, can send out my senses and find out where they are. The only one I can't locate would be Cole but he would survive it, and I don't care about sending a lump of concrete and tar on top of him right now whether he survived it or not. I leap down onto the roof, everyone staring at me in disbelief as I land gracefully on my feet from a fall that would kill any human. The rest are using climbing equipment to reach it. I send my senses out as a few men begin running to see if I am OK. I put my hand up to stop them and they freeze where they are, watching me with sorrow, assuming I'm one of the mothers with one of those freak adrenaline bursts I guess.

I sense nobody in the room beneath me and I punch a hole in the floor, wait a moment for the dust to settle and jump down. After a few minutes I'm joined by a group of men, all shouting back up the hole they have just dived down but all I catch is 'who fucking cares what she is our fucking kids are down here!' there must be some mixed views about whether I'm here to help or hinder, and those that have followed me look at me with a small smile as a thank you and run out of the room to look for their children.

The room looks as though it was abandoned centuries ago, chairs broken and covered with dust from the ceiling. Table tops an inch thick with it. But when I turn to see the chalkboard it gets really creepy.

You should have stayed with me when you I told you to
Everyday your gone a life is lost because of you.

I sense a group of children a few floors down, and I push my fears aside to follow my instincts. As I pass another room I have the most horrible urge to go inside even though I know what I will find. The handle is cold and rigid as though it was slammed so hard it shattered inside. I only have to push it slightly and the door creaks open, revealing a stench of death so strong I gag. I can't see anything at first and I try not to adjust my site to the darkness, but whether I like it or not my body automatically knows what to do. I take in the scene before me in a matter of seconds, and I scream in horror. The blonde hair is the only thing recognisable about the decapitated head on the ground, one eye ball hanging from its socket as the flesh has clearly been peeled away. The rest of the body cut into pieces and hung from what looks like meat hooks above the children's desks. And the worst part of the entire thing, is the bloody footprints on the ground clearly belonging to a child. This teacher was brutally murdered in front of a child.

    I run out of the room and feel about to pass out, if not for the instant clanging sound from the other side of the corridor telling me someone is watching me. I stand up and follow the sound giving in to the idea that I might die today, but determined to get the children to safety first.

    I walk steadily, waiting to find out where Cole is hiding. He must be inside the school, I feel drawn to it so he must be. I am crying as I wander the corridors, reduced to this after everything. As the shouts and screams and relieved cries make their way to me I relax and think of all the times I have been awake, hoping for distraction from what I have seen. I think of the souls I have met, the things I have seen, the places I have visited.

    I think of how humans take everything for granted. It was truly a wonder to walk this earth and when Humans fall, as you shall, as the magical creatures did, I had hoped to see what would be the next take over. Now I see no future for myself at all after finding Cole. I will end up that nameless faceless teacher in that room. I refuse to think about it anymore as children appear at the end of the corridor. Dirty, tear stained, bruised kids that all look like they have been through hell and back but are thankfully still walking. I am mesmerised by their smiles, children always have a smile hidden deep down even in a tragedy. And from somewhere inside me I find one for them. Giving high five's and hugs to the kids screaming with happiness that they have been found instead of crying about what they have been through. I suddenly realise I should be happy I ever knew love before my existence came to this. I now know my purpose is to sacrifice myself to save these children, and I shall accept it bravely.

    I watch the children from behind as they find their way to freedom, the teachers that have cared for them the last few days wipe away tears, looking shaky and weak. As they walk out of site I feel a tugging on my hand. I look down to see a girl. Barely able to stand, I catch her before she falls.

    "Mummy?" she breathes clearly struggling to see in the dim light. I cry again for her.

    "No sweetie I'm not your mummy. Let me help you find her." I begin to walk back up the corridor with her, being sure to avoid the room with the body inside, when Cole walks out of one of the rooms and stands before me. Instantly I move the child to stand behind me so he can not hurt her. She sits on the floor and leans against the wall for support, unsure what is happening but feeling the need to fear this man.

    "Violet, how nice of you to join the party." his voice is menacing, and I shiver with fear.

    "Cole, let me take her up to her mother and then I will come down to talk to you."

    "You didn't come to fight me?" he breaths in

surprise. The smile in his eyes is undeniably breath taking but I must focus on the task at hand.

"I couldn't if I tried we both know that. I am here to offer myself in return for them. Let me take this girl back to the surface and then I am all yours. Completely yours Cole, just please stop this madness. You can control me, not the world. But me." I beg him, and after hesitating for a few moments he moves out of my way. I cry with happiness and dread as I see in his eyes that he accepts. I take the girl in my arms again, but as I walk past him his hand latches onto mine and I yelp. His ferocious power is evident as he digs his fingers into the flesh of my wrist.

"Remember I can find you, come back here to me when you have finished." he spits with his words dripping acid. He isn't the Cole I love, I don't know where that soul is. This is a mad man in a demons body. This is dangerous.

"I will." I say quietly and he unwillingly lets me go. I walk away with the girl in my arms. As I am walking up the corridor I make sure the girl is unharmed.

"Are you OK?" I ask, she smiles at me.

"Thank you Violet, for saving us."

"You're very welcome, your parents are waiting for you and we wouldn't want to upset them anymore would we."

"You are going back to him?" she asks while trying not to fall asleep in my arms, I get the feeling this is the safest she has felt all weekend.

"I am. But don't worry about me, I don't need saving." I kiss her forehead lightly.

"Everyone needs saving sometimes." I choke on my tears at her words and in that moment I know she is an old soul. I don't awaken the soul, this child has been through enough. She just needs her mother and a good meal now.

When I reach the opening in the ceiling I hear voices, a woman's hysterical cries. "Go get her, go get her now! Find my baby! What do you mean she wasn't with the others?"

I shout up for someone to help and as I stand on a table and hold the girl up to the others, someone above grabs and pulls her through the gap. I hear the woman scream with joy and watch as the child becomes engulfed in arms, a woman's face appears looking down at me.

"Thank you, thank you so much. You saved my baby."

"Mummy she saved us all from the bad man, he won't hurt anybody anymore." the woman looks at me, unsure. Then she beams and repeats her thanks. She offers her hand to help me out but I shake my head. I jump off the table and make way down to Cole ignoring her shouts after me, she knows I helped her child and she wants to help me. But my future is this. Finding Cole so he won't hurt anyone any more.

When I find him he jumps up and grabs me. He seems nervous.

"I wasn't sure if it was true, or if I had imagined you. Are you really going to stay with me?" he asks with wide eyes.

"Yes Cole, I give you myself. IF you stop hurting and terrorising others." he looks shocked again but shrugs and, taking me by the hand, leads me out of the school via an entrance I didn't know existed. "No more killing."

"We are finally going to be together forever, you don't belong to nature any more Violet you belong to me." As he says the words he smiles, assuming I would enjoy hearing them. But I don't want to *belong* to anybody.

Chapter 16

"How are you doing this?" I ask Cole after we have been following the same cave for quite some time, when I turn my head to look behind me I see the walls of the cave knitting together showing no escape.

"I'm manipulating the rock. This is where my real life began, when I was brought back after my human life. I was very weak. I didn't know anything about what I was or where I was to go. I didn't learn to use my powers against the cold or pain until around three years after living in a cave by myself. The rock watched me struggle, waiting for me to find myself. None of the animals ever attacked me and now I know it's because they sensed what I am. I knew I couldn't die but in those dark times I wished I would. It was torture living that pathetic existence, always shivering from the cold and catching my arms and legs when climbing. I broke my leg once and had to be nursed back to health by a wild wolf!"

"It was only when I was at my absolute lowest, with memories of your death and the bitter cold attacking my immortal yet fragile skin that the rock of the cave opened up to me. I could feel it entering my mind and spreading warmth throughout my body, connecting with me and nudging me to use the powers I had neglected. Now I don't even need to try to use my power to stay warm or heal injuries, it's as though my body does it as natural as breathing." his words bring back the memory of me losing my breath at our passionate encounters, and I absent-mindedly wonder if I will ever feel the same way for this amazing, destroyed creature that is now keeping me as his prisoner, a mere possession.

"Shortly after the rock helped ease me into my abilities it introduced me to a very close friend of mine. Do you know the story of the Minotaur, Violet?" he turns to look at me walking behind him and I shake my head silently. His eye's gleam and sparkle as though a child with the chance to tell his favourite story to the rest of the class.

"Well, as you know legends and the truth are pretty far from each other, changing from one person telling it to the next and so on. The legend taught around the world now is that there was a great king, Minos of Crete. He was a very powerful king, feared by all of the rulers of the lands that surrounded his own magnificent kingdom."

"King Minos would demand riches and treasures and other goods from these smaller rulers and in return he would not wage war upon them. They say he built an extremely large Labyrinth, a maze of rock that stretched for miles and miles underneath his very palace. In the centre of this maze there lived a Minotaur. The body of a powerful man, fused with the head of a horned bull. This Minotaur loved eating flesh from human bodies. When he tired of his riches King Minos demanded the other rulers to send 7 young men and 7 young women every month to feed the Minotaur, to keep it happy and stop it getting lose and causing chaos in their kingdoms".

"The legend also says that the only man capable of killing this Minotaur was Theseus. He was given visions of the Minotaur's weaknesses from the gods, and thus was able to slay the beast."

Cole turns again to stare at me, and I can sense what he is going to say next.

"Do you see it? King Minos was a demon that

attempted his powers in such a way to change people into animals, he is the Demon that started werewolves as they call them now. He created the Minotaur by mistake, but grew to love it as though it were his own child. He manipulated the ground beneath his home to turn it into a cage for his hideously beautiful creation. Not to keep it in, but to keep others out.

"Nobody made it out alive, not only because of the Minotaur but when he sealed the victims in the maze he closed the rock afterwards. There was no door left to open, no escape to find. The boys were used to feed the Minotaur and the women were kept in cells made of rock, they were mated with the Minotaur to breed more." His eyes still gleaming even though there is no light to reflect. If not for our extra senses and abilities we wouldn't be able to see anything. But I can see, and I wish I couldn't. The excitement on his face while describing this tragic tale is purely horrific.

"How many did he create?" I ask with a croaking, hesitant edge in my voice.

"None of them survived." He shrugged as though it was nothing to worry about. "They were either killed during the mating process by the Minotaur, I can't see him having the gentlest touch can you." He laughed loudly at his own joke while my head started to spin with what he was telling me. "Or Minos killed them after repeated disappointment. None of them ever managed to carry a child."

"So they were just raped by a beast and murdered." I feel sick thinking of what people have experienced. Here I am complaining that I now belong to this creature and millions of people have suffered much worse fates. I feel instantly ashamed of myself.

"You will meet Minos later, although now he goes by the name of Milo. It's a little more up to date don't you think?" he turns and carries on walking not waiting for an answer, I follow behind not exactly enthralled by the idea of meeting him. My head bent down as I shuffle forwards, ashamed of myself and the Demon I wish I didn't love.

Eventually we arrive at a strange cave exit, the perfect view of the sea crashing down just meters below our feet. The entrance behind us closing and a sort of rock pathway forming along the edge of an enormous cliff, when I follow it with my eyes I see a wooden door randomly placed in the side of the cliff. Again I walk forward behind Cole only this time my head is up, gazing at the beauty of the smooth blue sky contrasting so strongly with harsh grey coloured rock at the top. My eyes fall back down to see Cole, magnificently silhouetted before the strong glare of the sun, he is standing in front of the wooden door awaiting me to open it, but I just stand there. I refuse to open the door on my own imprisonment.

He looks disappointed, but opens the door and pushes me inside.

"This is your home now Violet, you need to remember that." the threat in his words very clear, although I don't think he meant it to be there.

When I walk into the house/cave I am struck with a sight so beautiful it takes my breath away. I can't stop staring at the cosy and comfortable home he has made here. A fire roars in a corner with two great big arm chairs in front. Shelves upon shelves of books line one of the walls. A pile of books placed randomly on the floor between the chairs. Old fashioned oil paintings of boats and landscapes adorn the walls. Another door to the left shows there is more to see, but I can't stop myself from investigating one of the arm chairs. I was expecting a mansion with expensive artefacts scattered here there and everywhere, or a penthouse apartment that springs to mind from a book Veronica must have read, but instead this is extremely homely.

"The bedroom is through that door there, I know we don't need to sleep but I made it on the way back, for any other reasons you can think of." Cole leers at me and instead of doing what he wants and flirting with him, I merely take a book off the shelf and sit in one of the arm chairs. He seems annoyed but he doesn't voice it. I think he is angry with my silence and reluctance to be happy, but to scared I will leave to do anything about it.

"I have made a bathroom for you as well." he says pleading with me to be excited about that.

"Why Cole? I don't use the bathroom." I say bluntly.

"Didn't you enjoy the shower that night in the hotel? Wouldn't you like to go and have a shower now? Or maybe a bath even?"

"No thank you. I'm quite happy sitting here and reading." I answer his plea with refusal. He wants me to relax, as if I could!

"Well I'm going to run you a bath, then I really think you should try It." he is ordering me, all be it politely.

As he leaves the room I look back down to the book I chose, the hard blue cover with pretty patterns all over it. The words 'Wuthering heights' written elegantly at the top and the author's name, Emily Bronte, across bottom.

I'm aware of the sound of running water as I begin reading, desperate for some escape and distraction and quickly lose myself to the beautiful story. Before I know it I hear the door to the bedroom open again and Cole stands wearing just a towel, a strange grin spreading across his face.

"Come." he commands.

"I would really much prefer to read if it's all the same to you. Enjoy your bath." my voice is even, not rising or falling as it would were I caught up in emotion. The passion I felt for this man has gone, this is no longer a love story. This is slavery. I watch as his face falls with enough disappointment that would make any woman sob, yet I just pick up my book and continue where I left of. He stands for a moment in the door way trying to find something to say, but eventually he slams it behind him as he leaves me there alone. I hear banging around on the other side of the door and then silence. Thank full for some peace I slip back into a state of non-existence. For a short while I won't be Violet the ex-vampire turned prisoner of an evil demon, I will be whoever this book lets me be.

I sit with my hand on my heart totally enthralled in my book when I hear a slam, Cole barges out of the bedroom with a bag in his hand.

"A holiday!" he booms "We will go on a couples holiday. A romantic getaway just the two of us. Get a hotel, have meals, meet other couples it will be great! Where would you like to visit? Rome? France? Anywhere you want. The world is ours."

"You mean I can choose a different environment in which to be your prisoner?"

"Violet you need to come to terms with this sooner rather than later. You gave up yourself as a bargaining chip not me, I just accepted your deal. You should think yourself lucky I am willing to treat you so well." I stare blankly back at him wondering how he managed to come to that conclusion. "You are being ignorant, purposely awkward. I am trying to be patient with you but I have to be honest. I had hoped for better from you."

This time I don't even say anything to him, just shake my head in disbelief and pick up my book again. Before I know it he has taken the book from my hands and thrown it into the fire. I watch in momentary shock as the pages catch alight and burn to a crisp. When I turn back to look at Cole ready to yell and scream at him I quickly change my mind. He is angry. Frighteningly so.

"Get up. We are going." he says quietly, I snap my mouth shut and stand too frightened not to do as I am told. If Cole were to lose his temper with me, would I lose mine? It is bad enough that I am now his slave but I made a promise a long time ago to never be a slave to darkness. If I allow myself to be pushed too far, darkness will consume me the same way it is Cole.

I follow him out of the wooden door into the sunlight and again a pathway shows it's self within the cliff leading us to the surface. I hear sea gulls and turn my head in every direction I can to watch them soar through the skies, free as birds you could say. I can't help but to envy them slightly.

"Where are we going?" I ask quietly when we reach the top.

"Rome." he answers me with one word, and as I wonder how we will get there I hear a thundering noise bellowing all around us as the clouds darken and the wind picks up, only instead of above me it's below.

The sea begins crashing angrily against the cliff

face, the seagulls scatter and fly away as the sea splits into two before my very eyes, the rock beneath the ocean rising to form a magnificent walkway.

"Moses?" I whisper as the scene before me brings a flash back from Veronica's memories of being taught how Moses parted the red sea.

"Minos. We are going to his home." Cole smiles warmly clearly the moment back in the cave forgotten, I think he looks on this other Demon as a father from how excited he gets just to talk about him. "When Moses led the people to the desert, what happened next was NOT as the bible describes! The Ten Commandments however where correct. He had everyone believing him and made up these Ten Commandments so that humans might feel more inclined to cause havoc. We all know how irresistible it is to do something you have been told not to." he sniggers.

"We will walk." he says, answering my unspoken question of how.

"Will Minos mind us turning up to visit without planning it first?" I ask thinking how this is all like something out of a story book, and not a good one!

"He already knows we are on our way, the rock will have informed him." he answers simply. I still don't understand the connection with rock and earth. I was connected to earth as a warrior, I didn't think Demons could to.

I start to feel groggy after a while of walking and I worry what it could mean, my body is walking yet my head feels free. As though it could float off at any minute. I feel as though I'm falling, and when I let the feeling take over I am caught within warm and comfortable arms.

"I have freed our minds, it's a very long

distance and boredom takes hold after so long. I let your mind choose the memory we would visit and this must have seemed the best." I look around and see we are back in the hotel room in which we turned human and spent a passionate and lust filled night in each other's arms. I stretch my arm out to touch the table with a phone on it next to the bed, and I can physically feel everything. Cole's arm goes around my waist and he leans in to kiss my neck. No tingles. No breathlessness. I feel no emotion at all.

"Shower, now." he commands with I assume what he imagines is a seductive tone yet to me he may as well be barking orders, and the entire scene falls apart around him like a shattered picture frame. I am pulled back into my body with a shock as my legs continue walking the path through the sea like some kind of robot.

"Violet what the hell was that?" he seems furious.

"The night in the hotel was a night we were both free Cole, you took me back there as your prisoner. You ruined the memory, not me."

Chapter 17

"You can tell Minos we have arrived." Cole whispers into the air as he caresses a boulder when we reach land again. I believe this is more a warning for me than a message for his friend, he hadn't needed to speak out loud when he brought the rock from beneath the ocean yet he said Minos would know they were coming.

"There are no memories of this place in Veronicas mind."

"That's because Veronica was a human, and any human that finds this place is killed instantly. They call it the Bermuda triangle where weird and unusual things take place. Ships go missing, aeroplanes vanish all never to be heard of again."

"What happens to them?" I ask hesitantly.

"Minos created the Minotaur using a human and a bull. Must you ask?" I shudder to hear the truth of the situation. The man we are visiting could be harbouring all manner of abominations within his walls. After a few more minutes awkward silence we approach a small well hidden cottage, gigantic oak trees both tall and wide tower over the pathetic looking house and I let out a small chuckle.

"I wouldn't laugh at him Violet, remember that not all is as it seems."

Cole pushes the door open and I follow him inside, crouching through the small ill-fitting door. But when he moves out of my way I gasp and blink away from the brightness of pure white marble everywhere. Instead of a magnificent sweeping staircase as I had imagined there is just one simple looking elevator in the centre of the large room. Much larger than the cottage looked from the outside.

When my eyes adjust I see the gold metal rails of the elevator, like roots starting on the ceiling of the room and entwining down the walls to the centre of the floor where they begin to worm their way back upwards creating a sort of cage within. Cole tries to hurry me to the elevator but I can't stop myself from inspecting the elegant gold coloured patterns. Slowly, they raise from the wall at my touch and begin to ever so delicately wrap around my fingers, the whole thing looks so enchanting and mystifying I feel instantly angry when Cole pulls me harshly away. His only reply to my evil glare is to remove a button from his shirt and give it to the vines.

And they take it, wrapping lovingly around it in and out of the buttons little holes, I feel like dancing watching them intertwine like children playing a game in a field. But the gold vine like thing begins to tighten around the button. They pull it and grip it and tighten until the button falls in broken pieces to the ground, the vines below covering them and dragging them away.

"Wow that was intense." I breathe a sigh of relief as the elevator starts to move, clinging to Coles arm as though he is my saviour instead of my captor, which I hadn't noticed I had been doing. I let go when I see it also makes him feel uncomfortable but I can't tell if he is disappointed or confused.

"You better stay close to me while we are here." I smile at him slightly, desperately trying to hold back the school girl grin I feel spreading and instead turn to look away. My emotions and feelings have me all confused, how can I go from not feeling anything at all to clinging onto him for dear life within a matter of minutes?

The metal cage holding us clangs and clatters as we drop much quicker than any regular elevator would, but then I already assumed from the lack of any wires or buttons at all that this is very unlike any other elevator on earth. Eventually we stop in what looks like a whole new world. The sun is blaring, the gardens are beyond beautiful and flower beds stretch as far as the eye can see filled with flowers I haven't ever seen before.

"Beautiful isn't it? Minos saw what the humans would do to the natural beauty of the world and stole a piece of it hiding it down here for safe keeping. These workers are gifted with a swimming ability that lets them hold their breath for long periods of time. If they feel the need to reach the surface at all they take a swim in that pond over there, it has a secret tunnel. Most of these flowers and trees don't even exist on the surface anymore because of the pollution of humans." His words make sense but I can't help but curl my lip in irritation at the disgust dripping from his voice when he speaks of humans.

"It is not your place to judge them you know. Our kind had their chance too, and although we might not have destroyed the planet as they are now we still fell. Maybe our job now is to guide the humans. Maybe we failed where they succeed and vice versa. Maybe our real purpose in life is to find a happy medium."

Cole's head leans to one side as he seems to seriously consider my words, but he is quickly distracted by the booming thunderous voice coming quickly down between the flower beds towards us.

"I know they have arrived, no thanks to your

incompetence!" The woman by his side is clearly struggling to keep stride with him, but I am more bothered by the fact that this largely built man is racing his way towards me wearing only a red silk dressing gown that isn't even tied closed at all. I quickly avert my eyes desperate for anything else to look at instead of the extremely offending view ahead.

"Cole my good friend, you have brought me a gift?" His eyes roam freely over my body from top to bottom and back again making me instantly feel dirty and afraid.

"She is mine." His hand reaches out and grabs the top of my arm, and I choose to think of it more as a protective grab than proof of ownership.

"I see, if you feel like sharing you know where to find me." He turns on his heels making the dressing gown fly upwards and giving a perfect view of his completely naked rear end.

"Oh Maranda here will be your handmaiden. It will keep her out of my hair for a while at least!" his tone sounds harsh as though that will be her punishment. I go from being angry at one pompous demon to another when Cole simply throws his bag at her and begins dragging me with him. I snatch my arm away and turn to Miranda.

"I will carry that sorry, I'm Violet." I say politely hoping for a friend. She curtseys as though I am the queen!

"I know who you are ma'am all is ready for you. Please let me carry your bag while you take in all the garden has to offer."

"Violet your being rude!" Cole actually snaps his fingers and points to the floor in front of him as though he is calling a dog.

"I can't help it, I tend to mimic the company I keep." My eyes shoot daggers at him but I quickly remember my place when he starts marching his way back towards me and grasps me again.

"Remember who belongs to who, I would hate to have a lovers tiff so early in the relationship." I see Minos waiting and quickly bow my head, falling in step behind Cole.

"She needs training Cole, I could do it for you. I have more than enough space in the dungeons for one more." I am sure Minos is drooling at the thought yet I refuse to bring my face up to look at him, or his appendage desperately trying to catch my attention.

"I am not yours to train. I answer only to Cole, that was the arrangement and that is what it will be."

"How dare you be so disrespectful in someone else's home!" Coles hand connects with the side of my face and I fall to the floor, the burning in my cheek seeming to set off the other dangerous kind of burning sensation and I close my eyes against the fury, blocking it out completely so I don't lose my temper.

"Have the maiden take her to my room if you please Minos, I will give her some time to think about what she has done and how lucky she is." He turns and walks away leaving me there on the ground.

"Miss?" Asks the quiet and broken voice of Miranda, when I look up I see she is a very young woman standing with her head bowed as though embarrassed to have witnessed the scene.

"I am Cole's prisoner."

"Ma'am please follow me to your room." I stand and walk behind her suddenly curious as to who she is and how she ended up here at such a young age.

"What is your name?" I ask.

"You may call for me as Maid." She answers almost stiffly.

"I didn't ask what I may call for you as, what is your name."

"My name is Maranda." She seems to speak as though afraid her voice alone would offend me and it breaks my heart.

"I'm not the enemy here, you don't have to watch your manners around me." I say the words softly thinking this young woman could help me, maybe she could be a friend while I am here. She stops walking and turns to face me with her face still lowered to the ground.

"I don't mean to cause you offense miss, but I do not wish for a beating today. I must show you to your room and then finish my jobs."

"Well then let's walk and talk."

"I am just the Maid." She turns and walks briskly up the stairs for me to run following behind.

"You look like a person to me."

"With all due respect miss." She sighs heavily before carrying on. "If I could be anything in the world, a person would be last on the list."

"What does that mean?"

"You clearly don't know many people." She shudders as she opens a door and steps back allowing me entrance. "This is your room, if you need anything else just yell 'Maid' and I shall appear. It is one of the spells Minos put on the room for your arrival."

"I'm sure I will be just fine, I wouldn't want to cause you a beating just to straighten my sheets." I had hoped for my words to be gentle and kind and perhaps even make her giggle, but I can't help but panic when she runs into the room flustered and begins pulling at the bed sheets.

"Apologies if they aren't to your liking Miss I really tried to get them straight, I was so busy I must have missed a few creases." She blusters around the bed clearly about ready to pass out in fear thinking I was serious about the bed sheets being ruffled.

"Miranda!" I say harshly as I grab her shoulders to stop her. "The bed is fine, I was trying to make a point. I am sorry for upsetting you."

"What is this?" Minos's voice from the doorway has us both jumping and the young girl scurrying to leave the room, but his arm flies out to stop her causing her to wince away in fear. "What are you doing inside the room?" he asks her menacingly.

"I…. I was just straightening out the sheets sir. They had come ruffled in one edge."

"You let a guest into a room with ruffled sheets?"

"No she didn't, I ruffled the sheets when I sat on the bed and Miranda kindly came to straighten them back out for me."

"You are a bad liar." He accuses with his finger pointed harshly at me, his free hand flies to the young woman's face and she howls in pain. He keeps his hand attached to her skin for a moment forcing me to stand and watch in horror as whatever he does to her forces her to her knees screaming in agony. When he removes his hand a red blistering handprint remains on her face and she cries to herself as she bows to him and walks quickly from the room.

"Do not talk to the maids again, someone else will have to pick up her failings today and that means something else around here doesn't get done. I will hold you responsible next time." Minos moves out of the way showing Cole was stood behind him the entire time and didn't do a thing to help. Maybe helping Cole find the goodness inside him will be much harder than I anticipated, impossible even.

Chapter 18

Cole wakes me the next morning by roughly shaking my shoulder, he had wanted me to sleep in the bed beside him but I crept onto the floor in the middle of the night when he was fast asleep was unable to shake the uneasy feelings I get when I'm near him, torn between love for the man I could lose if I'm not careful and hatred mingled with fear for the demon taking over.

"Fall out of bed did you?" His voice sounds disappointed, almost begging me to agree with him so he would know I didn't leave his side intentionally. I just stand and start to look for my clothes, struggling holding onto the black silk scrap of material I had wrapped around my body like a towel the night before when he throws another pile of material my way. "Wear this." I hold it against my body and look at my reflection.

"It's the same as what I'm wearing now, just in a different colour." I look at him with confusion, wondering if he really expects me to wear this all day. "How am I supposed to wear this?"

"Like this." He holds the piece of material out and shakes it roughly before gathering it in the centre and twisting it in his hands, draping it over my right shoulder to cover my front and back in white shimmery silk, as I let go of the black material from underneath it slinks down my legs to the ground. The gold coloured rope on the bed makes its way around my waist to act as a belt. He manoeuvres the fabric over my body until I look like some kind of Greek goddess. His fingers brush against the skin of my neck and I breathe in shakily, his hand stills on my shoulder as he watches me in the mirror clearly aware of my reaction.

The material falls away from my leg, showing more flesh to draw his attention and I watch as he licks his lips gently, seductively. His fingertips brush against my neck again, his other hand working down to my thigh and pushing the material further off my leg to caress my skin. I lean back into him and shiver slightly as I feel myself being pulled into him. He manipulates the strap of material he had formed moments ago to fall down my arm making both shoulders exposed, and pushing it further to expose my breasts. The sudden rush of cold air over my nipples makes me moan and I know there is more pleasure to be had, I have never felt so exposed and yet so liberated. I feel him harden against my back and the thoughts in my mind have me biting my bottom lip as I feel his teeth graze the skin of my shoulder, his hands working up to my breasts as my own arms make their way up to his head and invite him to explore my body.

"You look amazing like this, so powerful and spiritual. Like a goddess." He whispers into my ear as his hands rub my breasts again. A groan escapes my throat and he leans his head into my neck and roughly bites the flesh. My knees buckle as I cry out with pleasure. He spins me around roughly, full of animalistic hunger and kisses me, his tongue entering my mouth and making me forget everything going on around me as he heaves me against the mirror, my legs wrapping around his hips as glass shards fall to the floor unnoticed by the two inhuman beings about to tear the room apart.

"When you are quite finished destroying my

belongings breakfast is served." The voice comes from the doorway, and Cole drops me to the ground landing in all of the broken glass. I yelp and hop my way over to the bed while covering my body, all the time feeling Minos's eyes burning into me. I start picking out the pieces of glass knowing they will heal instantly yet still annoyed.

"Certainly, we shall join you soon my friend."

"Has your girl apologised for yesterday yet?" he asks harshly.

"No she has not, but she will be punished accordingly you can be sure of that."

"Have her apologise now for me." Minos is deliberately trying to appeal to Cole's evil side, and I start to get a glimmer of why he is so conflicted.

"Minos why do you have to do that? You know you will anger her, it's give and take man you know that." I smile to myself finally hearing Cole speak up for me against this vile disgrace of a being, but I can tell it won't last long. Minos has been Cole's friend and teacher for years, there is a bond there that won't be split over night.

"The girl has turned you soft my friend." Cole sighs and turns to me with a strange faraway look on his face and I am not sure he wants to do this. He looks apologetic.

"Violet, you do owe Minos an apology."

"Yes I do." I say with slanted eyes. "I'm sorry you can't make your own dam bed and have to get some young woman to do it for you. I'm sorry you can't stand the thought of an outspoken woman and instead of listening to what she would have to say you feel the need to silence her. And most of all, I'm sorry for the gaping hole in your soul you wish to fill and so obviously aren't doing a great job of as you still feel the need to make others feel inadequate. Basically, I'm sorry that you are a prick." I say it in my most sincere voice, with a very serious look on my face, and am met with laughter from Cole and an almost excited glare from Minos.

"You will have to keep a close eye on her my friend, I might be tempted to have some fun with her myself."

I make my way out of the room following Cole and Minos and wonder if I had missed a pair of sandals or anything while getting dressed.

"Cole?" I ask and he slows down so I can catch up, I link my arm in his feeling much more comfortable than the night before, safer almost with him around, and walk gently at his side. "Was I supposed to put some shoes on? I think I must have missed them." I feel almost embarrassed to ask, I place my hand on my chest more for comfort reasons than anything else but I notice his eyes following my hand.

"Women do not wear shoes here, yesterday you had just arrived so I couldn't expect you to know my rules but today you will start to learn how things are done here." Minos's voice booms without him even turning around to look at me. Cole just nods his agreement without taking his eyes off my chest, I smile inwardly as I start to see a way I can control him.

"Oh, why is that?"

"Because my dear, my power comes from the rock you are walking on. The rock surrounding you at this very moment is filling me with everything I need to survive and thrive for centuries. It doesn't get the power from nowhere you know."

"So, you are draining the life from the women

that live here?"

"I am draining the life from every woman on the planet. Women are very powerful beings, they can create life from the seed of man and experience the intense pain of childbirth and feel nothing but love afterwards, women are the best energy source on this planet."

"And yet you abuse them." my words halt Cole with an expression on his face as though to say he had never thought of it like that before, and in an almost cute way he seems to avoid looking at my chest.

"Excuse me?" Minos's voice seems agitated and I can't stop myself but to carry on.

"Well you have just admitted that women are extremely powerful, and much more important than men in the role of giving life and nurturing, and you take the energy from these women to fuel your pointless existence on an island that nobody can even get too. It sounds to me like you should be building a shrine and worshipping women, giving back something after you stole it. Karma." I finish with a confident smile and Cole seems extremely proud, until I fall to the floor screaming in pain.

"How dare you express that opinion in my house, how dare you openly mock me in front of my slaves. Worship women? They can't even behave properly. The gifts were given to the wrong sex. I take your power because you are not worthy of it, petty human woman daring to attempt to make me out to be a fool." My womb feels as though it is about to tear from my body, twisting and pulling inside me as though he has it in his very hand.

"Minos no, you don't even know who she is!" Cole warns torn between worry of what I might do if I let the vampire out, or what will happen to me if I don't.

"She is a fucking woman Cole, you need to learn how to control her!" he shouts and snaps his fingers, sending Cole soaring backwards into the wall.

"There is something you should know about me, Minos, I only belong to Cole because I sacrificed myself as the first vampire to save the lives of others." I reach my hand towards him and squeeze, he instantly drops to his knees not able to breath. "I don't like doing this, I find it hard to stop myself taking things too far with darkness, when I try so hard to be perfectly balanced. I can take a slap when I haven't behaved 'appropriately' for a slave, and I can take evil eyes and randy glares with a pinch of salt. But do not think that I will sit and politely accept while you try to control me. I belong to Cole. I am his. I will tear you a new asshole in your throat before you get close to torturing me."

He whimpers on his knees with his hands encasing his manhood which is yet again on show to everybody, just as when we arrived. The stream of red appearing from between his fingers as I grasp his balls from meters away making me smile and with one crunch I sever them entirely. He is a demon, he will heal straight away. But I hope he heals with a new life lesson. Cole reaches my side and takes me hand, staring at me in awe with more than adoration on his face.

"We could rule the world." He grins.

"That wasn't the deal." I say softly and turn away from him.

Chapter 19

Minos has been staring at me strangely all day and I think it has something to do with my new fascination with the phrase *grow a pair*, I can't help but feel as though letting him know who I am and what I am capable of has unleashed something inside me that won't be bullied or belittled. His attitude around me has changed, instead of his usual demeaning and ignorant behaviour with walking around naked suddenly Minos is at my side eager to show me his palace and fully dressed. I feel like he is showing respect for what is probably the first time in his existence.

In the gardens he was beside himself trying to find the best smelling flower, the juiciest fruit, the fountain where the water ran the clearest, and the most extravagant statues. Yet what impressed me more than anything was Cole snatching me away into a bush, and showing me a river made by nature flowing through the trees. Of course when Minos found them he quickly manipulated the ground to get rid of it, clearly not accepting that nature alone can make more beautiful scenery than he can. I can tell everything about this demon is competition and he isn't used to losing.

"Violet come see this." Cole's voice echoed through the grand entrance hall when we returned from our walk, he was pointing to the painting on the ceiling and we almost fell apart laughing at the copy of Michelangelo's famous painting Creator of Adam, only where god normally laid on a cloud was Minos and he was touching the finger of his Minotaur.

"He thinks himself a god?" I ask through hysterics.

"Am I not entitled to that?" He is standing at the top of the stairs watching with crazy pride. "God is a creator is he not? I created the Minotaur. Legends are spoken of my creations all over the world. Even the werewolves, although they failed at the time, are spoken of today, glorified even into being a teenage dream much like the vampires are. This haven I created, is it not a world of its own? I create life, therefore I must be a god."

"We are going to go for a little rest in our room Minos." Cole says loudly after a moment stunned silence, and he quickly rushes me up the stairs past him, trying not to laugh too loudly as we run around like imps in a forest.

"I would like to see Violet sometime later, would you meet me in the drawing room in an hour?" He asks me.

"I don't see a problem with that." I feel Cole stop walking, his hand tugging mine as I try to keep moving.

"What do you want with her?" he asks Minos.

"I simply wish to know a little more about the vampires. Call it curiosity." Minos shrugs as he turns away from us.

"I don't trust him, he is up to something." Cole breathes.

"I don't think we have anything to worry about." I chuckle remembering the last time Minos tried anything and tug Cole to our bedroom.

Ever since I unleashed my power onto Minos I have seen a new light in Cole, it is as though reminding him I could easily leave at any time, but don't, has brushed away most of his evil side. I wonder if it is because Minos is too busy trying to get on my good side to bother trying to manipulate him anymore. Or maybe when he was afraid I would leave him he let the darkness consume him believing I would be too afraid to leave. I think I have managed to get past most of the darkness and show the real Cole that for as long as he is acting like a prison warden I will feel like a prisoner, and the more I feel like a prisoner the more I will want to leave.

We enter the bedroom and quickly begin making ourselves more comfortable, flopping onto the bed as though we are exhausted. Cole props his head up on one arm while lying on his side next to me.

"Violet, something's changed. The last few days I have felt happier than ever before. Do you think you could tell me what's happened?" he traces the fingers of his free hand on my bare shoulder as he talks.

"Well. I am your slave. I have vowed to stay by your side for as long as you don't hurt other people." He looks almost hurt. "A few days ago the thought of being someone's slave had me almost wanting to take my own life, if only I could. All I had to look forward to was a lifetime of torture. But now, I don't feel like a slave. In the last few days I think you have come to see me as someone to love, and I have seen your constant turmoil of evil versus good. The truth is I forgive you for what you have done, because I think you need me to keep you balanced. I think I am your salvation, and I hope when I have saved you that you can do the same for me." I give him a few minutes to digest my theory yet when his fingers move to gently stroke my lips I feel like he hadn't even heard me. Instead of getting upset I lay my hand on his. "I don't think you're as bad-ass as you think you are."

I screech with laughter as he dives for me on the bed, rolling quickly away as he pretends to be too slow to catch me, teasing me to think I might actually get away, I hide in the bathroom and lock the door laughing to myself.

"When I get in there you are in for a world of pain Violet, I'll teach you a lesson you will never forget!" His fist pounds on the door as I hide in the shower behind the curtain giggling to myself, and when he finally uses his powers to manipulate the lock I see his excited face all lit up with delight through a small gap. I shrink into the shower biting my lip in anticipation.

"AAARRRRRGGGGHHHHHH!" I scream laughing as a blast of cold water launches from the shower head and drenches me causing me to jump out of the shower. The guffaw of laughter behind me having me turning with an evil glare that only lasts a few seconds. The look on Coles face stops me in my tracks as his eyes devour me, and when I look down I see why. The cold water has made the shimmery material completely see through and stick to every inch of my body showing my curvy figure beautifully. Cole marches forward and seizes me in his arms, kissing me with more passion than I ever knew anyone could have for another person. My hands are in his hair, my tongue deep inside his mouth begging for him as he wraps his hands around me, pulling me towards him until he reaches the sink where he shuffles his body until he is sitting down over the sink. He hoists me up with my legs bent at either side of him, his mouth only leaving mine to whisper my name.

I lift myself up from sitting on top of him and

try to take his shirt off, but he takes my breast in his mouth and starts playing with the nipple between his teeth, his hands holding my waist roughly.

"Stop!" Cole looks up at me groaning with annoyance. "I have go see Minos remember." I slide down his body and he just watches me as I look around for a towel and quickly begin drying my hair as best I can.

"You don't have to." He says with worry in his voice.

"Cole I love you like this." My hand reaches up to stroke his cheek, and he kisses it and leans into it. "I don't want evil to consume you. I want to take you away from evil and be together. Like this. Please, let's go?" I ask him hopefully and I see him battle the idea in his mind.

"We can't just leave now it would be rude!" he says but the way his eyes roll from side to side tell me he is trying to think of a way we could.

"Then we will stay, but I must go and see Minos." Cole clicks his fingers and Maranda appears.

"Help Violet get dried, I am going for a drink."

"I didn't know you drank."

"I need to do something!" he says as though it should have been obvious, I turn away from him confused but giving him space so not to make him angry. When he leaves I smile at Miranda, guilty that I had forgotten about the injury I caused her. Not that she could forget with the hand shaped burn mark on her face.

"I am sorry!" I say desperately to her.

"Ma'am?" She asks not sure what I mean.

"I tried to help you, but I just got you in more trouble."

"Please Ma'am it was not your fault. I needed to

learn my place."

I bite my lip to try and stop myself from crying, and I reach out to brush her hair off her face. When she flinches I feel instantly ashamed.

"I'm sorry again, I wasn't going to hurt you. I promise." I lift my hand slowly and watch as she closes her eyes, afraid to watch as she believes I will beat her. I brush the stray strands of hair behind her ears and tilt her head upwards, and she opens her eyes to look at me with fear. "You can't be more than fifteen years old!" I whisper.

"Apologies Ma'am, did you want someone younger? Or perhaps older and more experienced?" she shakes again.

"I want to know how you are here working as a slave when you should be out there enjoying your life!"

"With all due respect Ma'am I know what Minos's visitors want in this situation, and I would very much appreciate if we could just get this over and done with."

"You are shaking with fear. What do you think I will do to you?"

The only response I get is a tear down her right cheek, her left still blistered and I assume the tear duct is too damaged to work.

"No." her eyes close tightly and she begins to sob. "Oh my dear Miranda please say they didn't!" I wrap my arms around her to give her a hug, she doesn't respond but I don't expect her too. With the kind of man I know Minos to be already she probably thinks I'm trying to lure her into a false sense of security.

"Sit down dear." I say and offer her the stool by the bath tub, she sits down hesitantly as I sit on the side of the bed through the door.

"How did you get here?" I ask her warmly.

"I was a failed experiment." She sobs.

"Excuse me?"

"My mother is downstairs in one of the chambers, Minos used her in one of his experiments but instead of birthing a super human species she birthed me."

"Super human species?"

"Yes. He has been experimenting more with human cross breeds."

"So you are part human and part?" I ask curiously.

"Fairy. My father was a human, my mother is a fairy."

"Oh wow."

"It's the only reason she is still alive. He kills all the human women who fail him, but it is hard to find other souls these days."

"So your mother is locked away in a chamber?"

"Yes under the palace. Everyone knows about it, he sends us to fetch them sometimes."

"How many champers are there?"

"One for each experiment."

"Which is?"

"Twenty seven. Each holding around five to ten beings. If it's all the same to you Ma'am I have other jobs to be doing." She says nervously clearly wanting to be anywhere except here talking to me.

"Of course I am sorry Miranda, but please call me Violet. And I promise you, I am here to help not to hinder." She tries to smile warmly at me but I can tell she still isn't sure about me. I quickly stand up and start looking for something dry to wear, I have to go and speak to Minos.

Chapter 20

"Hello? Minos?" I ask entering the drawing room, taking in the rows upon rows of books and making a mental note to return here for some time alone when I get the chance.

"Violet!" He beams appearing from one of the chairs facing the opposite direction. "Join us." He insists. I instantly feel on edge, as though something isn't right. The entire atmosphere seems to go cold and unwelcoming sending chills up and down my spine, I try to shake the feelings off and tell myself I am imagining things.

"Have you seen Cole? He said he was going for a drink a while ago." I suddenly have the strange urge to find him and keep him close, a fear of being alone with Minos. I can't help but think nature is trying to warn me of something.

"Nope not in here, come in." I try to find an excuse to stay standing by the door, already feeling uncomfortable and on edge.

"I should really find Cole, he seemed agitated when he left and I want to make sure I haven't angered him."

"Oh he will be fine, don't worry about him he will get over it! Come join us, we must talk."

I walk towards Minos to see who is sitting in the chair next to him and I recoil in horror, sinking to the floor and sliding away.

"I thought it was about time you meet my son." He points to the other chair, the beast in all his glory sat naked before her.

He was easily the size of three of her, crouched

into one of the tub chairs with his animalistic legs covered with fur and ending in hooves curled back on themselves as he looked extremely uncomfortable. His almost human arms ending in stubs with metal rings welded to the end sitting at his sides with nowhere else to go, no space to shift around for comfort at all. He looks like an elephant squashed into a mole hill. His face difficult to judge since it wasn't human, but his eyes are black, his tusks and horns covered with dribbling saliva from his grotesquely malformed mouth entwining together and piercing back into his flesh to protrude in all angles and just offensively in my direction. I fall to the ground in shock, backing away from him as he breathes heavy and fast. The only thing human about this beast is the fact that he is sitting in a chair.

"Please take a seat." Minos mocks pointing to a chair opposite, but I can't take my eyes from the Minotaur. "I was wondering how much you knew about me. You know that I created the Minotaur, and that I experimented with other human and animal mixtures all of which failing. But I wonder if you knew about my other experiments?" he asks.

"I now know you are experimenting with other beings, fairies and the like."

"I wondered how long it would be before she spilled her guts! Well I think it would only be appropriate for me to spill her guts. I shall make a mental note to punish her later. And you can enjoy knowing that when I slice her flesh apart and pick at her insides to feed my boy, it will all be your fault."

"Don't you touch her that poor girl has been through enough!"

"You don't know the half of it!" Minos laughs out loud menacingly while pouring some more of the brown coloured liquid from the small circle table by his chair into his glass before throwing the empty bottle into the roaring fire. "She is starting to wear a little thin now though to be honest, she has been used too much and I have had my fill. Or should I say *she* has had my fill!" again his laughter booms in the large room echoing off the walls and shelves.

"You're a monster!" I spit.

"Oh thank you my dear but I really want to get off the subject of me now. You see I want to talk about you." His eyes light up and I fear I might already know where he is going with this. "The women I have been using; humans, fairies, wolves and such, have all been disappointing. They are not strong enough to perform the tasks I need of them. But you? You will do perfectly. Now as we all know the Minotaur is definitely the most powerful beast in this room, and the most successful out of all of my experiments. I had hoped to try a few experiments with his offspring but thus far this task has proven impossible. Human women died from his beast like mating so I was forced to try other methods, and although the other beings I found survived, they never conceived. They were never strong enough!" his lip curls as he speaks as though this thought physically disgusts him, and I find I have never hated anyone as much as I hate this soul.

He stands from his chair and I see he has removed his clothes again, the silk dressing gown gaping open as he walks towards the desk at the other side of the room, taking a seat behind it.

"Now I would give you two some privacy but I have to admit, I have thing for watching." He winks at me as I still subconsciously attempt to shrink my body and become less of a target. "Go get her son!"

he booms, the Minotaur stands revealing his true size, and I scream with fear grasping my heart almost painfully.

When he stands it is very obvious that while he is alive and very powerful, this being is clearly in a lot of pain. His grotesque appearance is due to him basically being a freak of nature, an experiment thought up from this monster of a man and carried out into existence, torturing this one poor soul for eternity. There is no understanding at all apart from basic commands I see, he doesn't know this is wrong because nobody cared enough to teach him. This poor soul has never had a chance at life and not just because of his physical appearance, but because his creator never wanted him to have a chance. He only ever wanted a weapon to use however he saw fit, not caring about the effect any of it would have.

"The Minotaur is not your son, he is the tortured warrior you hide behind!" I scream and stand up, feeling the burn of furious darkness start in my toes and creep up my legs to wrap around me, comforting me. "I will kill him, if only to save him from you!"

The doors to the drawing room burst open and before I know what is happening Cole is barging into the Minotaur, knocking him over and distracting everyone in the room while he repeatedly stabs the beast with a knife he must have carried with him just in case. He knows he doesn't stand a chance against the monstrosity, but he is willing to sacrifice his life to give mine a chance. I sense the darkness has left him and I feel I owe it to him to try not to lose myself. Minos starts to move into action until I let the burning take over my body, trying desperately to keep it out of my mind.

"Minos you are being judged here and now."

My voice is amplified as I rise above the floor, I feel tendrils of fire creeping along my body and I welcome the power they lend to me knowing there is always a price. "You are to be punished for your crimes, against souls of all species."

The Minotaur throws Cole off as though he is a mere doll and slams him into the floor, his claws spread out like a pitch folk piercing through his torso as Cole screams out in agony. I try to block it out knowing I can heal him after this has ended. I reach my hand towards the Minotaur and imagine I am taking hold of his heart, I mentally caress it with my fingers in the hope to show him at least a little warmth before his death, and then I squeeze it to nothing. The darkness obeying my unspoken commands like puppets on strings, eager and excited for the kill. A quick and painless death for a beast who was never supposed to be here.

Minos runs towards me with anger in his eyes, spittle flying from his mouth as he growls like a demented animal and screams at me to bring him back and change what I have done. I merely spread out my hand towards him, manipulating the darkness to hold him in a type of cage, I picture in my mind the gold vine like patterns from the room with the elevator and somehow they appear in the room worming their way over to him as they creep upwards and form the same cage as before only where there was an elevator now cowers a whimpering demon.

"I heard you when you came here, you told Cole that it isn't his place to judge. You're a hypocrite. Let me out of here!" he demands although his voice shakes and I feel he is trying to act much braver than he feels.

"It might not be my place to judge you. But then

it fits doesn't it? It wasn't your place to play with nature, to create beasts, to take prisoners and have them raped and killed, to sit back and play your little games with other's lives. So I agree it is not my place to judge you, but I'm going to do it anyway."

I step towards the cage and begin to stroke the vines with the backs of my fingers showing them the appreciation I think they beg for, and I gently whisper to them not to let him out. Then I quickly make my way to Cole who is still on the floor in a puddle of blood.

"Time to get up now Cole, it's all over."

"I'm afraid it's not as simple as that." Cole struggles for breath, holding the holes in his chest that aren't healing. "The Minotaur was a beast, a powerful one! Nobody could survive the injuries from his claws. Minos enchanted them to such an extent that it is near impossible to heal from them. Even demons struggle with the help of a little darkness." Cole smiles softly to me, and I can see his smile is supposed to say *I'm sorry* and *I love you* and even *Thank you* as he brushes my cheek.

"No you can't give up, this can't be the end!" I place my hands over his wounds and begin to heal him knowing I have more darkness ready for orders than any demon, but he pushes my hands away wincing in pain. "Let me heal you!"

"No way! It took me long enough to get over the pain of letting the darkness take me, you helped with that. You will need to take more power from it to heal me, and I won't let you do that. It is too risky. You saved me. Now it's my turn, remember?"

"No" I beg him.

"Yes. We are saving each other. Maybe in the next life, we will be together." With those words he seems to physically shrink in my arms, deteriorating into just a shadow of a man.

Miranda enters the drawing room and screams, not knowing where to look. She runs over to try and help with Cole but I wave her away.

"Free everyone!" I yell at her. "Go to the chambers and let everyone out. You are all free." She seems confused for a moment but hurriedly runs away to do as she has been told. I turn back to the cage holding Minos. "Your punishment is simple, I strip you of all your powers and turn you human."

"Then what are you going to do to me?" Minos asks from his prison in the centre of the room.

"I'm not going to do anything to you, I haven't earned that right." He sighs in relief as I let the cage fall around him, releasing his human form.

"Then I hate to break it to you but that's not much of a punishment. What's the catch? I have to promise to be good?" he raises his eyebrows in a joking way.

"The others in the chambers however…." I leave the sentence unfinished and revel in the fear in his eyes for a moment.

I take the ornamental letter opener from the desk and with a cry of emotional rage I ram it through my own heart, drowning out the screams as Minos understands the extent of what he is to expect from his victims. Stripped of his powers and let loose on those he tortured while trapped on an enchanted island where he will never be helped.